Moved by the Whispers

PART 1

K. L. HUNTER

Copyright © 2025 K. L. Hunter

All rights reserved. No part of this publication may be reproduced, distributed, or transmitted in any form or by any means, including photocopying, recording, or other electronic or mechanical methods, without the prior written permission of the publisher, except in the case of brief quotations embodied in critical reviews and certain other noncommercial uses permitted by copyright law. For permission requests, email the publisher:

Attention: Permissions Coordinator
Welcome To The Storm Publishing!
info@midnightstorm.net

Ordering Information:
Quantity sales. Special discounts are available on quantity purchases by corporations, associations, and others. For details, contact the publisher at the email address above.

Library of Congress Control Number: 2025905317
Orders by U.S. trade bookstores and wholesalers.

ISBN: 978-1-966612-19-3

Cover Design: Amman WPDesign

Veronica Miller, Red Diamond Editing by V. Rena,

reddiamondediting5@yahoo.com

First Printed Edition: June 2025

Printed in the United States of America

FOREWORD

"Family should be the place where you can be your most complete self. Where you're accepted and appreciated, seen and valued, even in the moments of disagreement. It should be your soft place to fall, the place where you're reminded that no matter what happens to you, in the face of your deepest challenges, you are loved."

— OPRAH WINFREY

I was more afraid to start college than I was to start kindergarten. A young child doesn't know how much there is to be afraid of. Everything feels exciting. A high school graduate, however, has just enough experience to see where fears can take shape. Lucky for me, the first person I met as a freshman at The University of Alabama in 1994 was LaTisha Hunter.

Maybe it was her welcoming smile or her contagious laugh. Something about LaTisha made me think, *we need to be friends*. That was nearly 30 years ago, and I'm so grateful I listened to that instinct. Since then, LaTisha and I have only deepened our bond, especially as I've met the other important people in her life. Through her, each of us has come to know what it feels like to experience true connection. We understand loyalty in its purest form, and we've weathered countless storms, knowing she was never far away.

Moved by the Whispers is a story that embodies that same care and closeness. It's a tale of a tight-knit group of family and friends growing together, showing up for one another, listening, and offering support. Their lives intertwine, and as they do, they come to see each other in new light. Through their journey, they learn that relationships should never be taken for granted and that loss is an inevitable part of life.

LaTisha is the best kind of storyteller. She surrounds you with beauty and brings her characters to life in such a way that you can't help but become invested in their journey. As I got to know the people at the heart of her novel, I couldn't wait to see how their story unfolded. I found myself wondering how they would unravel the mystery that binds them together. How would they confront one another's secrets? What would happen when characters used to their predictable patterns are forced to embrace the power of belief?

Each chapter left me craving more, and in many ways, I saw glimpses of my own family, my friends, and even myself in the pages. *Moved by the Whispers* is fiction, but it is packed with truths that remind us to trust our intuition and to find our voices. Through its pages, the reader is gifted with the strength to look inward, and perhaps, the courage to say, "I'm sorry. I forgive you. I love you."

This book is an invitation to contemplate the love we share with our family of origin (or the family we choose). There is a mystery behind the story that brings this family together, but it's also a story of love. LaTisha has shown me the power of compassionate connection for decades, and I have no doubt *Moved by the Whispers* will hold similar revelations for you.

Andora Hinton-CEO, Willow North Growth Partners & Lifetime Friend!

CONTENTS

PROLOGUE 2
CHAPTER 1 4
CHAPTER 2 12
CHAPTER 3 19
CHAPTER 4 22
CHAPTER 5 26
CHAPTER 6 33
CHAPTER 7 40
CHAPTER 8 50
CHAPTER 9 63
CHAPTER 10 72
CHAPTER 11 79
CHAPTER 12 91
CHAPTER 13 99
CHAPTER 14 104
CHAPTER 15 112
CHAPTER 16 114
ABOUT THE AUTHOR 122
ACKNOWLEDGMENT 123

K. L. Hunter

"Your life is always speaking to you in whispers, guiding you to your next right step. And in many situations, the whisper is also the first warning...."

— OPRAH WINFREY, THE PATH MADE CLEAR: DISCOVERING YOUR LIFE'S DIRECTION AND PURPOSE

PROLOGUE

"Did you hear that?" Trinity asked, her eyes scanning the room.

"Hear what?" Carmen replied, looking around in confusion for whatever Trinity was referencing.

"Well, if you didn't hear anything, I guess it was nothing," Trinity scoffed.

"Girl, I swear you're always thinking you hear something. Why are you so paranoid?" Carmen teased.

Am I being paranoid? Trinity thought to herself. *But I could've sworn I heard someone say something.* She tried her best to shrug off the feeling, but then she heard it again—*Move*.

This time, Trinity stood up from the table where they were sitting and walked toward the bathroom. Just as she did, the waitress who was passing by spilled all of the drinks right where Trinity had been sitting.

"I knew it! I knew it!" Trinity squealed, unable to contain herself.

Not realizing she had verbalized what she had been thinking, Carmen raised an eyebrow. "Knew what?"

"Don't tell me you somehow knew that the waitress was going to spill drinks all over our table. Is that what you heard?" Carmen asked, a hint of disbelief in her voice.

"No," Trinity snapped. "I'm not crazy or psychic," she muttered, feeling embarrassed. Or was she?

Trinity knew she had heard a voice, and what she just witnessed seemed to confirm that. But how could she explain this to anyone without them thinking she was insane? *I might be better off keeping this to myself,* Trinity thought.

And at that moment, she made the decision to do just that. But at what cost?

Chapter 1

It's October 2014. The air was crisp, but the sun was shining brightly. Trinity Gorden wore a bright yellow sweater and jeans, and her hair had the cutest yellow and white bows tied to two long plaits—one on either side of her head, running past her shoulders. It was a style she didn't readily appreciate, as she felt it was far too childish. I mean, she was ten, after all. Yet, Trinity's hair was always the talk of the other moms, who often asked if her dad was really her dad, or what else she might have in her because full Black folks don't have hair like that. She'd learned quickly to disregard their comments and stares, because her mom always reassured her that she was the cutest thing ever and that she was most special. So special, in fact, that it snowed the day she was born. Now, that was definitely an anomaly, seeing as they lived in Florida—yet, not enough to stop her from wondering if her mom truly knew she was different.

Trinity always felt she was different but wasn't quite sure why. She looked like the other girls, yet there was this feeling that she never fully belonged in the group. This was a profound feeling for a kid, and one she was not completely capable of deciphering on her own. There were times when she wondered if something was wrong with her, or if she just truly had an overactive imagination. But the things she experienced could not be blamed on an overactive imagination. It couldn't even be blamed on some type of mental deficiency. Or could it?

She attempted to speak with her mother, Delores, about it on various occasions. But, in true mother fashion, she would tell her to just go be a child and not to worry about being different, because everyone was different in one way or another. However, despite knowing that everyone was different in some way, Trinity knew that her difference was on a whole other level—a level that she had been running from since she was five. At least, that was the first vivid memory she can recall of having the feeling, hearing the voice, and seeing the results of the aftermath. Until today.

While out playing with her best friend, Camille, Trinity had a very eerie feeling she could not quite explain. I mean, she's ten, and who was going to believe that a ten-year-old had a premonition? Especially since she didn't know the full definition of, nor had she heard the word "premonition" used often. She certainly could not explain it. Nor could she tell them that this wasn't the first time. All Trinity knew was that she and Camille needed to go inside—and they needed to go right now. So, she stood up and told Camille that they should go and play inside, but Camille was having so much fun that she didn't want to go. Trinity pleaded, but Camille was determined not to go.

Just as Trinity began to sit, she heard a voice say, "Tell her you have cookies inside." She looked around because she knew she heard the voice, but there was no one there but her and Camille. Then she heard it again, but this time, it was stern. So, Trinity told Camille that her mom had made fresh cookies, and they should go inside. This delighted Camille and off they went into the house.

Just as Trinity closed the door, she heard tires screeching and then a loud bang. Her mother began to frantically call her name as she ran into the kitchen from the living room. As soon as she saw Trinity and Camille, she grabbed them both and asked if they were okay. They both shrugged her off and said they wanted cookies, but Trinity noticed the fear in her eyes and asked what was wrong. Delores tried to play it off, saying that she had just awakened from a bad dream, and sent the girls to wash their hands. But Trinity knew something was wrong. She took a step but looked back and asked her mom what the loud noise was that she'd just heard outside. But her mom simply said for her to go wash her hands and that she would bring the cookies to them in the playroom.

As Trinity and Camille washed their hands, they began to hear sirens blaring. They looked at one another and ran toward the front of the house. Right before their eyes was the most horrific thing either had seen. Camille instantly began to cry and ask for her mom, and Delores quickly scooped her up, consoling her as she walked out of view of the scene. She beckoned for Trinity to follow, but it was as if she was planted in place. The cars were tangled together in the very spot that she and Camille had been playing in the front yard. Was this why she had the feeling of going inside? Was this why she heard the voice? A single tear fell from her eye, and she ran to her room to cry without anyone knowing because she was afraid. It was an unusual kind of fear. Not a fear that would prevent action, but a fear that made you uneasy because you had so many questions. It was this fear that moved Trinity into a full-on cry fest.

Apparently, after much time had passed, Trinity woke up from a cry-induced sleep on her closet floor, covered with a blanket. This could only mean that her mom had found her there. She opened the closet door to find Camille asleep on her bed, covered in a blanket that matched hers. Trying not to wake her, she tiptoed out of the room and ran smack dab into her dad, Andrew.

"Hey, Muffin!" he proclaimed very loudly. Muffin was the nickname he had given Trinity as soon as he knew Delores was pregnant.

"Hi, Daddy," Trinity mumbled into his neck as he scooped her up for one of his famous and all-too-welcoming bear hugs and walked down the hallway toward the living room.

"How was your day, Muffin?" he asked as he plopped her down on the sofa next to him.

Having flashbacks of everything that had happened, Trinity only whispered, "Okay."

"Just, okay? It had to be more than okay because I see your best bud, Camille, is here," exclaimed Andrew. "Come on, tell me what's wrong."

Trinity sat quietly for a moment, and just as she filled her lungs with air to tell her dad about the feeling, her mom walked into the room.

"There you are," she said with a smile. "I went back to your secret place, and you weren't there. How was your nap?"

"It was good, Mom," Trinity said with a smile. "Can Camille sleep over tonight?" Trinity figured this would help take her mind off of what happened earlier.

Delores looked at Andrew, and they both said *yes* to Trinity's excitement.

She immediately jumped up and ran down the hall, repeatedly screaming, "Camille, Mom and Dad said you can stay over," until they could no longer hear her.

"She's such a doll," Andrew said with a smile, to which Delores agreed with a simple nod.

"She is certainly that! But I hope today's events don't torment her, Drew," Delores said with a look of concern.

"Ahh, Dee, she's going to be fine. Look at her. They were both in the house before the accident happened, and while apparently shaken at seeing the wreckage, I think they are both going to be alright. Don't worry. Let's just be thankful to God that our darling daughter and her friend are okay."

"By the way, have you spoken to Carmen and Curtis about what happened today?"

"Yes, I called Carmen so that Camille could speak to her because she was so upset. I'll let her know that Trinity wants Camille to stay, so she and Curtis don't have to worry about rushing back from Tampa tonight."

"How's Curtis' mom doing?" Andrew asked.

"She's still hanging on, but the doctors are saying it's just a matter of time."

"Have they told Camille and Cayden yet?"

"No!" Delores declared. "Those kids love Retha, and this is going to devastate them."

"I know, I know," Andrew said while rubbing Dee's shoulders. "But don't you think they need to have a conversation with them to prepare them? I think it would be even harder to deal with if they just showed up for a funeral and see their Gigi laying there."

"They're ten and eight, Drew. How do you propose they have that conversation?"

"Calm down, I was just saying that I thought it would be easier for the kids to digest. There's no need for this to cause a disruption in our marriage."

"You're right, I'm sorry. I guess I'm still just a little wound up from today's earlier events. Drew, our baby and her friend could have been killed. It's like Trinity knew the exact moment to come inside. If you could have seen the look on her face when she saw the cars in the yard... it's like she just *knew* she had been saved."

"So, what are you saying, Dee? That Trinity has some kind of superhuman power? That she knows things before they happen? Seriously, Delores, I think you've been watching too much of that TV show. What's it called?"

"*Manifest*," Dee whispered.

"Yeah, *Manifest*. But Drew, you didn't see her face, and I'm not saying that Trinity is psychic. I'm saying I just feel that she had a sense something was not right."

"Okay, enough of that. Here, take this glass of wine and relax. I'll get the girls to come have dinner."

"Wow, Mom, these chicken tenders are stupendous!"

"Yeah, Mrs. G, they're stupendous," Camille said with a laugh. "And so are the Brussels sprouts. I know most kids hate these things, but I love them."

"Ugh, you can have mine," Trinity exclaimed.

"Oh no she can't. You're going to eat your veggies, young lady."

"But, Mom," Trinity groaned, "I've already eaten three of them. Surely that counts as an attempt. That's what Dad always says."

Dee looked over at Drew with a raised eyebrow. "Oh, does he now? Well, if you can eat three, you can eat seven because you have four more on your plate."

"Seriously??"

"Enough, Trinity. Eat your veggies or no dessert, period."

"Yes, ma'am," Trinity said with a sullen look on her face.

As Dee and Drew began to clear the table, Camille kicked Trinity.

"Ouch!!"

"Shush," Camille exclaimed with her finger to her mouth. "Give me your Brussels sprouts," she whispered.

"Okay," Trinity giggled and handed them off one by one until they're all gone.

"Mom! Mrs. G! We are ready for dessert!" Both girls glibly shouted.

Deloris looked at Andrew and smirked. "They really think they're getting over on me."

"They certainly do," Andrew laughed as he grabbed his slice of cake with ice cream and walked away.

After eating their desserts, the girls readied themselves for bed and a quick bedtime story.

"So, what is it that you girls would like to hear tonight?" asked Deloris.

"How Noah built the ark!" shouted Camille.

"How you know it's God speaking to you?" said Trinity, softly.

Her mom asked her to look up and repeat herself, but Trinity simply said, "Let's go with the Noah story."

It was at *that* moment Deloris knew.

Her heart began racing at lightning speed, and she could feel the sweat bead up on her face. This was the last thing she wanted for her daughter. It was more than a notion that she herself had to endure - the many visions, voices, and carnage. Well, technically, carnage wasn't the final result of her *episodes*, as she called them. Until that fateful night. A night that she tried to leave forever in the darkest crevice of her mind.

Why now, she wondered? It had been at least five years since she had an episode. That was until today. The day she realized that her daughter also had life-altering premonitions.

"Lord, if you please, don't allow Trinity to experience what I experienced. Allow her to always be obedient to your voice. Amen," Dee whispered before turning off the bedroom light and pulling the door close to Trinity's room.

Chapter 2

The next few weeks were rough for Trinity. She noticed everything. She felt everything. But she wasn't sure why, and it was making her very sensitive. So much so that Camille said she was being a crybaby, which only made her even sadder than she already was.

"I am not being a crybaby. I'm just overly emotional," Trinity said with a pout.

"But for what reason?" Camille asked. "You've been looming around like you lost your best friend. But, umm, hello! Here I stand in the flesh," Camille mused.

Trinity laughed as she pushed Camille towards the bus. "Come on here before we miss the bus, silly girl."

Just as they got to their usual seat, Keisha popped up from behind. "Hey, girl, hey!" Keisha was one-fourth of the mighty force known as "Friend Girls for Life" (FGFL).

"Listen, I forgot to tell you at lunch that Catrina said she was not going to make it for the annual FGFL day out next Saturday."

"Why?" Camille asked with a frown.

"She didn't really say, just something about it not being a good time, but she'd make it up to us."

Trinity leaned over to peer out the window, but she didn't see the typical scenery. She saw Catrina leaning over a casket, and Camille, Keisha, and herself were standing behind her, trying to hold her up. But as quickly as she saw the vision, it was gone.

"That was odd," she said.

"What was odd?" Camille chimed in, which startled Trinity as she didn't realize that she had verbalized the thought.

"Oh, just that Catrina can't make the outing but didn't say why. Maybe her Dad is taking her on a day trip to Tampa or Boca Raton. Who knows, honey?" Keisha said with a pop of her tongue.

"Who knows, indeed," Trinity whispered before leaning back into the window to peer out until the bus reached their stop.

As she stepped off the bus, Uncle Todd met her, and she immediately forgot that she was sad. Todd was like the big brother she never had, didn't really want, but needed all the same.

"Hey, Peanut!"

"Hey, Uncle Todd. What did you bring me?"

"Hey there now. Why is it that you always think I have something for you?"

Trinity laughed and pulled away from Todd as he tried to grab her ponytail.

"Because you always do, so what is it this time, dude?"

"Oh, so now I'm 'dude' and not Uncle Todd. I see, I see. You think because you're my favorite niece, you can treat me any type of way."

"Uncle Todd, I'm your only niece!" Trinity squealed.

"Hmm, I guess you have a point," Todd chuckled. "Let's get inside and we'll see if I have anything for you. Besides, it's cold out here."

Once inside, Trinity dropped her coat and backpack on the floor because she heard a familiar voice. She looked up at her Uncle Todd with bright eyes and asked, "Is that Nana Jean?"

"Sure is," Todd said. "I drove all night to get her here before you got out of school."

Nana Jean was Deloris and Todd's mom, and she lived in Tennessee. But every year, she would make her way to Orlando to stay until April. They called her a snowbird. She said she did it because they acted like they didn't know their way home anymore.

It was true that Deloris and Andrew rarely visited Nashville anymore, with Deloris making the most excuses as to why they never came home. Drew would persist from time to time but would eventually leave it alone when he noticed Dee withdrawing and becoming reserved.

"Nana Jean!" Trinity squealed as she ran into the living room and jumped into her lap.

"Easy there, Muffin," Drew said while steadying her on Grandmother's lap. "Nana Jean is not a toy, and she isn't as young as you."

"Watch your mouth," Nana Jean retorted. "I may be 66, but I'm not out of commission yet."

Everyone laughed, including Trinity, as she asked, "What's out of commission?"

"Oh, don't you worry about that, little one. You just keep living, and time will tell you." Nana Jean smiled. "Now tell me about your school day and what's been going on with you and Mimi."

That was Nana Jean's nickname for Camille.

"Well now, let's see. Where do I start?" Trinity began.

"My oh my," Nana Jean chuckled. "I might need to get my things in order before I hear this story. Help me to my room, and then you can fill me in on all the good stuff."

"You bet," Trinity said, jumping up, ready to go.

"How is it every time I see her; she has more energy than the last time?" Todd quipped.

"Just be glad you don't experience it every day," Drew replied.

"Interesting," Dee said. Todd and Drew turned to look at her with perplexed expressions.

"What do you mean?" Drew asked.

"Todd asked about Trinity's energy, and you said be glad you don't experience it every day."

"Yeah?" Drew said.

"But you don't experience it every day, I do."

Todd burst into a full-on belly laugh, much to Drew's dismay. "Ah, now, babe, don't throw me out like day-old greens. You know what I mean," he said as he grabbed Deloris around her waist and pulled her in for a kiss.

They all laughed and headed toward the kitchen.

"What's for dinner?" Todd asked. "Because your little brother is hungry."

"You know your mom only wants to stop for gas, like she's the one driving."

"Oh, so now she's *my* mom," Deloris teased.

"If I recall, she just purchased you a new Dodge Charger."

"Look!" Todd said, "That's beside the point. You know how Mom gets when she travels."

"I do," Deloris said. "Which is why I let you go get her every year."

They both laughed as Deloris opened the fridge door.

"Once again, you've knocked the ball completely out of the park, Dee," Todd said with a satisfying grin and a rub of his stomach. "That coconut curry chicken with cilantro lime rice was hitting on all cylinders."

"Yes!" everyone exclaimed.

Dee thanked everyone as she excused herself from the table and began removing dishes.

"Oh no you don't," Nana Jean said. "I'll clean the kitchen. You deserve to rest after putting it down like that."

"I guess I really did teach you something after all," Nana Jean continued. "Because Lord knows you couldn't boil water when you were 12."

This prompted everyone to laugh, even Dee, as she looked shockingly at her mom.

"Wow, Mom, I guess a thank you is in order. But from the amount of shade you just threw me, I'm wondering if I should grab my floppy hat and a margarita instead."

"You can grab what you want, honey, but truth is truth," Nana Jean said. "I always prayed you'd marry rich because the cooking skills you displayed at twelve were certainly not going to win you any husband."

Nana Jean got up from the table, and Dee just shook her head at her mom and her over-the-top candor.

Nana Jean shuffled into the kitchen and began to tidy up. "Hey, Lexa, play 'Distant Lover' by Marvin Gaye."

Nothing happened to Nana's chagrin.

"Why won't this thing play?"

"It's because you said her name wrong, Nana," Trinity quipped.

"So, her name ain't Lexa?" Nana asked.

"That's what your Uncle been saying for the past three days."

"It's Alexa, Nana."

"Well, Lexa, Alexa, Lexus, she knows I'm talking to her. Can't anybody else just start playing music up in here?"

Trinity giggled and walked over to the Echo Dot. "Alexa, play 'Distant Lover' by Marvin Gaye," she said, and instantly, the room filled with the melodious music and the sweet vocals of the late and great Marvin Gaye.

"Now this is music right here," said Nana Jean. "Not that rah-rah, drop it, shake it stuff y'all listen to today. This music has substance and heart."

"Don't we know it," said Drew as he scooped up Trinity and began swaying back and forth. "This is how I swept your mom off her feet," he told Trinity as she laughed.

"Uncle Todd, have you swept anyone off their feet?" Trinity asked.

"Naw, Peanut. Uncle Todd is a pl—"

"Hush your mouth," said Nana Jean. "Don't go teaching our sweet angel your devilish ways."

Everyone laughed as Todd said goodnight and headed out the door.

As everyone disappeared to their rooms to sleep, Deloris stole away to her reading nook. While sipping on a cup of warm peach tea, she began reflecting on her life. She realized that, in comparison to others, she had a marvelous life. She was married to the most handsome and attentive man ever. She was a stay-at-home mom but ran a successful handmade jewelry business. Her daughter was an excellent student and was involved in numerous activities: swimming, ballet, tennis, and violin. She was even a member of the GREATEST sorority ever created—Delta Sigma Theta Sorority, Incorporated! Deloris chuckled and let out the softest whistle in recognition of her love for her sorority.

But as quickly as the chuckle came, it dissipated. Deloris often wondered how she could have been so incredibly blessed when she thought back to that fateful night so long ago. A night that could have been so different had she just listened to *the voice*. But listening would have required her to accept the calling. Now she was being forced to address what she tried to hide for years because she knew her daughter had it, too. But Deloris knew helping her daughter was going to take her back to a place she didn't want to go and to reveal secrets she long thought was buried.

Chapter 3

"Merry Christmas!" shouted Trinity. "It's time to rise and shine. Come on, everyone!" Trinity burst into her parents' room and jumped into the bed. "Get up, Mom and Dad! It's Christmas, and I'm ready to open my presents!"

"Okay, okay," Drew answered groggily. "Give Mommy and me just a few minutes, and we'll meet you in the living room."

"Yay! I'm off to get Nana Jean up!" Trinity jumped off the bed and started singing, "Frosty the Snowman," as she trailed out of the room.

"I swear, we just went to sleep," said Drew to a wearied-looking Dee.

"That's because we did," she answered in her sleepy voice. "I'm still not certain why you insist on buying her things that require us to stay up into the wee hours of the night to assemble."

"Ahh, now, it's not so bad. Just wait until she sees it and her face lights up. Then you'll know it was worth it."

"Yeah, yeah, whatever," Dee said as she climbed out of bed and headed toward the bathroom. "Get up! We have about five minutes before she's back in here demanding our presence."

"Yup, I'm up," said Drew as he pushed back the covers and grabbed his robe.

By the time Dee and Drew made it to the living room, Trinity was in full present-opening operation.

"Wow! Looks like someone couldn't wait a moment longer," said Drew.

"Dad, you and Mommy were taking way too long," Trinity chirped. "So Nana Jean said I could go ahead and start opening my gifts."

"I sure did," Nana Jean replied. "Besides, looking at the number of gifts under this tree, she won't finish until next Christmas."

"I swear, you guys buy this child way too many toys," Nana Jean said.

"Huh," Dee scoffed. "Says the person who sent a list a mile long of things we needed to buy her just from you."

"Well, I'm the grandmother, and that's what we do," Nana Jean said as she sashayed toward the kitchen. "I need my coffee."

As they were watching Trinity open her gifts, Dee drifted off in thought.

"Come on, girl, you need to hang with us tonight," Joyce said to Dee.

"Girl, I can't come out with y'all because I need to study for this calculus test. You know Mr. Hunter's test be mad crazy."

"No, you're just scared that Thee..."

"La, la, la, la!" Joyce jumped in, successfully cutting Patricia off before she finished the name. "We don't talk about him."

"O," Patricia whispered, as the name was still on her lips before Joyce stopped her.

"Oh!!!" she exclaimed after realizing why Joyce had done what she did.

"Sorry, girl," Patricia said, rubbing Dee's arm. "I didn't, I wasn't, I'm..."

"It's okay," said Dee.

"Actually, it isn't," Joyce quipped, "but Dee is just too nice to tell you that."

"But I was only joking," Patricia said.

"Yeah, but you tend to do that too much," Joyce retorted.

"Now, look," Patricia said in a tone that changed the atmosphere, "you're not going to talk to me as if I'm your wayward child or something. I said I was sorry and that I was just playing around. If Dee has an issue with anything I've said or done, she is quite capable of speaking up for herself."

"Hey now," Dee jumped in as Joyce began to push back from the table. "Let's all just settle down. Joyce, thanks for feeling that you needed to say something. Patricia, I know you were only joking, and it's okay. I mean, the breakup between Theo and I is still pretty fresh, so it still stings, but I know you weren't trying to hurt me."

"Okay, see, everything is right with the world again," Joyce said. "So, can we get back to the situation at hand? Am I going to blow off studying or not?"

At this point, they all began laughing.

Chapter 4

"Hello. Earth to Deloris. Hey, are you still in there?" Drew asked as he gently shook her arm. "Mommy, what's wrong? Why aren't you saying anything?"

Deloris took a deep breath and smiled as she realized she had completely drowned out the present and gone way too far into the past. She plastered the biggest smile on her face and slid onto the floor with Trinity while locking eyes with Andrew.

"I guess I fell asleep, kiddo."

"With your eyes open, Mommy?"

"Yes, with my eyes open. You want to know why?" she asked while pulling Trinity into a hug.

"Why?" Trinity asked.

"Because your Dad and I had to help Santa put all of your gifts together last night and didn't get into bed until 3 o'clock this morning."

"And then you came bouncing into the room at 5," said Andrew.

"Well, the early bird catches da worms," said Trinity as she wiggled out of her Mom's embrace.

Everyone laughed, and Trinity looked perplexed and a little sad.

"Don't laugh at me," she pouted.

Nana Jean, still grinning and sipping her coffee, said, "Baby, that is not how that saying goes exactly."

"Yeah, hon," said Trinity with as much righteous indignation as her little body could muster. "That is what Paw Paw used to say."

"That's because your Paw Paw never had his teeth in, Sugah. You're supposed to say, 'The early bird catches the worm,'" her Nana explained.

"Ohhh," Trinity smiled. Then she frowned. "Paw Paw didn't have no teeth? Then how in the world did he eat, Nana?"

"That's *any* teeth, young lady," Dee corrected.

"Come here, chile," said Nana Jean. "You are mighty inquisitive, and it is way too early for all these questions. Let's finish opening these gifts, and I'll tell you later about all of that."

Everyone laughed as Trinity quickly gave a salute to her Nana and said, "Aye, aye, Captain," then quickly resumed opening her gifts.

"Hey you," Drew said while grabbing Dee as she stepped out of the shower. "What was really going on earlier?"

"What do you mean?" Dee asked as she kissed him lightly on the lips.

"When you faded to black on us this morning."

"Oh, that." Deloris tenderly pulled away and grabbed her robe. "I was just really tired, that's all."

"You apparently were as well, as you napped for three hours, sir."

"Hmm, so you want to deflect, I see."

"How is that deflecting?"

"Come here, grumpy," Dee laughed as she grabbed Drew and wrapped her arms around his waist. "You are so extremely cute when you're grouchy. Let's see if I can get you in a better mood."

Dee began planting kisses all over Drew's face and neck while caressing his back. Drew let out a slight groan and whispered in Dee's ear, "You're going to start something you can't finish."

"But what if I can finish?" Dee whispered back.

Drew scooped Dee up in his arms and headed into the bedroom. "Let's see about that," Drew said as he softly laid Dee onto the bed and lowered himself down onto her. He planted flowery soft kisses on her neck, just at her collarbone, and Dee purred with excitement. Drew slowly made his way down to her breasts, giving each of them adequate attention, which resulted in Dee arching her back and moaning his name. Drew took the hint, used his knee to spread her legs, and then he stopped. Dee opened her eyes with a look of question in them, to which Drew responded with a kiss and said, "Look at me," as he slid into her, and they both groaned with pleasure.

"Good morning, Mr. Gorden. You presented me with an absolutely amazing night last night. One I'm sure I will remember for a lifetime."

Andrew smiled and placed a sleepy kiss on Deloris' cheek, saying that she wasn't half bad herself.

"What are your plans for today?" Dee asked as she rolled out of bed, grabbed her robe, and headed into the closet.

Drew pulled back the covers, slid into his slippers, and put on his robe. "I was planning to go play golf with Curtis, Todd, Jerome, and Kevin. Did you need me for anything? I can reschedule if so."

"Oh no," Dee said as she emerged from the closet with her planned outfit for the day. "Mom and I were planning to go to lunch and have pedicures at the spa today."

"What are you doing with Trinity?"

"She's spending the day with Camille."

"How lucky are we to have a child-free day?" Drew said. "It's like licking the spoon full of cake batter."

Dee chuckled. "Pure heaven!"

"Heaven indeed," Drew said as he stepped into the shower.

Chapter 5

"Trinity, are you feeling better?" Camille asked. "I was never feeling bad," Trinity said. "Well, you've been acting kinda weird the past few months."

"Oh, it was nothing. I think it's just raging hormones. At least that's what Nana Jean said."

"Hormones?" Camille snorted. "What the heck are raging hormones?"

"I have no clue, but apparently it's a thing."

"But seriously, girl, you've been weirding me out lately. Are you sure you're okay?"

"I promise I'm good. I guess the realization of heading to middle school next year, finding out that Catrina's dad is sick, that accident..." Trinity stopped and looked up at Camille.

"Yeah, that was pretty bad. I still have nightmares sometimes. I mean, would we still be alive if you hadn't insisted we go in for cookies? Like, for real, girl, that was traumatic."

"Okay, I guess that kinda makes sense because I've been wondering about those same things."

"And like my dad always says, you have to extend grace because everyone is going through something."

"He's right about that," Trinity said with a wave of her hand.

"Sorry, girl, for thinking you were losing your mind."

"Ah, girl, it's all good. I mean, what kind of friend would you be if you didn't show concern about me? I'm glad we talked about it because I thought I was the only one feeling that way. Especially because you, Keisha, and Catrina seem like nothing bothers y'all."

"Trust, there is plenty bothering me," Camille said. "Like, how in the world is Catrina the youngest out of the four of us and she has already gotten her cycle?"

"I know, right?" Trinity said with fake astonishment. "But if I'm honest, I think I can wait forever for that. You see how moody she gets when it's that time."

"Yeah, but I also see how much her boobs have grown and how Reggie looks at her as if he could just melt. I want someone to look at me like that."

"You have someone," Trinity said.

"Who?"

"Your parents," Trinity said out loud and fell over laughing.

"Ooh, you are not so funny," Camille said through gritted teeth.

"You got a lot of great toys for Christmas," Trinity said to Camille.

"Yes, I did. My favorite is my Easy-Bake oven. Mom and I made a cake yesterday, and she said we could make cupcakes today."

"Ooh, cupcakes! That sounds fantastic because I love cupcakes."

"Yeah, so do I."

"But guess what I love even more?"

"What's that?"

"I love you, my best friend!"

"You are so funny," Camille said as she started to pick up her toys to put away. "We have to get ready to go to ballet class."

"Okay," Trinity said, but she was a little sad that Camille laughed at her expression of love. *Why would she not accept me telling her that I loved her?,* she wondered. *Mom and Nana Jean said I'm supposed to tell those that I love that I love them. "Give them their flowers," is what Nana always says. I was only trying to give them to her.*

Trinity shrugged it off and began helping to pick up the toys they had managed to pull out while playing. But she made a mental note to ask her mom and Nana about it later.

"Get into position, girls," the ballet teacher said. Camille, Trinity, and the other girls lined up at the barre and awaited further instructions.

"First position and plié down—one, two, three, and up—two, three. Again."

"Very good, Trinity and Catrina, very good. Shoulders back and down—one, two, three, and up—two, three. Nice, Camille and Keisha. Let's move into second position and plié."

The teacher continued until she'd completed all five positions. "Excellent warm-up. Now, let's get into our places for the first dance for the recital."

Trinity, Keisha, Catrina, and Camille opened up the first dance for the recital, and they were super excited.

"Come on, y'all," Keisha said excitedly.

They jumped into their places and gave their customary FGFL wink to one another. As soon as the music started, they blossomed into the stars they rightfully were. Demi plié into a coupé, followed by dégagé, sauté to passé, ending with a pirouette. They completed the combination again and ended with four entrechats before running offstage while the other dancers were entering the stage.

"Great job, girls, great job. Continue practicing at home, and I will see you all on Thursday. Please be sure to bring your permission slips with you if you plan to attend the outing to Orlando Ballet's adaptation of *The Nutcracker*."

"Yes, Madam Bufford," the girls replied.

All the girls exited the room and into the viewing area where their parents waited.

"Mommy, did you see us?" Camille asked, beaming with joy.

"Yes, I did, Angel. I see the FGFL was doing their thing tonight on the dance floor."

The girls giggled as they put their cover-ups on over their leotards.

"Mrs. Smith, we were throwing down," Keisha said with a laugh and a snap of her little finger.

"We sure did," said Trinity. "I can't wait until the recital. We are going to be amazing."

About that time, Keisha's mom, Stacy, walked up. "Thanks for waiting with Kee Kee until I got her, Carmen."

"No problem, girl, anytime. Besides, the other three-fourths of FGFL would not have let me leave her."

"Now you know I know," Stacy said as she took Keisha's bag, and they all walked toward the door. "Are you planning to chaperone the outing on Saturday?"

"No, Curtis and I will be in Tampa visiting his mom and finalizing some things there." Stacy gave her a knowing look, as she had just lost her father about six months ago.

"Deloris and Nana Jean are going. What about you?"

"Yeah, I plan to help out because you know these kids are going to be a handful."

"Yes, honey, they sure are, and I hate I'm going to miss it."

Stacy said she planned to give Deloris a call to see if they wanted to ride together since the girls would be on the bus.

"I'm sure she would be willing to do that, especially since we all live in the same subdivision."

"Alright, honey, let me get these girls home."

"Okay, see you soon, and tell Curtis hello."

As Carmen turned into the subdivision, she looked into her rear-view mirror to see that the girls had dozed off to sleep.

"Wake up, girls, we are home." Neither of them budged.

"Girls. Camille, Trinity, come on and wake up now."

Again, nothing.

Carmen drove through the security gate and around the roundabout before making it to the stop sign. She turned left to head to Deloris and Andrew's house and pulled into the driveway. As she put the car in park, Andrew walked out and met her at the car.

"Hey, Drew," Carmen said.

"Hey, girl, what's up?"

"Not much, just bringing your little lady home from ballet class. Apparently, class wore them out because they are both asleep in the back."

"No worries," Drew said. "I'll scoop her up."

"Thanks so much for letting her hang out with Mimi today."

"Now you know we couldn't keep these two apart if we tried."

"Ha! You're right about that. What time are you dropping Mimi off on Friday before you and Curtis head to Tampa?"

"She's getting off the bus with Trinity, and I'll drop her clothes off to Dee around lunch."

"Cool. Listen, you know if you and Curtis need anything, you better not hesitate to let us know."

"Thanks, Drew, we truly appreciate that. You guys are family. Especially with both of us being only children and Mama Retha being the last parent that either of us have. This is going to be especially hard, so if you can, be sure to reach out to Curtis a little more often. I'd definitely appreciate it more than you'd know."

"You got it, sis."

"Well, let me get home and get this one to bed. Tell Dee and Nana Jean hello."

Backing out of the driveway, Carmen heard Camille murmur in the background, "Hey, Pooh! Did you have a good nap?"

"Yes, ma'am," Camille said, still groggy.

"We'll be home shortly."

Carmen took a right at the stop sign and coasted down the hill past four houses, then turned into her driveway on the left. She pushed the control to open the garage and pulled in. As soon as the car stopped and the garage door closed, Cayden ran out.

"Hey, Mommy!"

"Hey, baby."

"Guess what? I got my black belt today!"

"Cool!" Carmen exclaimed. Camille jumped out of the back of the car and immediately asked Cayden if she could see the belt.

"Sure thing, sis, come on to my room and I'll show you. I had to break a board," said Cayden excitedly.

"A board?" Camille looked puzzled.

"Yep, I'll show you. I asked if I could keep it, and my sensei said yes."

The two trailed off into the house and closed the door, leaving Carmen to get everything out of the car.

"Lord, these kids," she said as she gathered everything and headed inside.

Chapter 6

"Time is flying by swiftly," Deloris said to Carmen. "It sure is. I can't believe we are already two weeks away from summer break. The kids are already talking about vacation trips and sleepovers."

"As if they don't sleep over every other weekend," Deloris chuckled.

"Well, Drew's brother is bringing the boys down sometime in June, and he said that he, Curtis, Todd, and Jerome were taking them on a camping, fishing, and hiking trip for a week."

"I remember Curtis mentioning that," Carmen said. "Is this the same week that the girls go to their Summer Intensive at the Orlando Ballet?"

"Yes, it's the same week. I'm so excited that all the girls made it this year," Dee stated.

"Yeah, me too. Stacy said that Keisha and Catrina were devastated last year when they didn't make it past auditions."

"I didn't know that Catrina didn't make it," said Dee. "I simply thought she didn't audition because it was so soon after Wayne passed."

"Apparently, they both auditioned and didn't make it."

"I think Catrina not making it had a lot to do with Wayne passing, as it had only been a month. To not know your birth mother and to lose your father just as you're turning ten is a lot for a kid. I'm just grateful that Wayne asked Stacy and Terrell to take guardianship of her so she would not go into the system," Dee explained.

"I always wondered about that," exclaimed Carmen.

"Didn't Wayne have siblings?"

"Yes, he has a sister and a brother, but they were estranged. He was his mom's only child, but his father had two additional kids. I don't think Wayne really spent time with them past his teenage years. Heck, they didn't even attend the service, I don't think."

"No, no," said Carmen. "I do recall now that his sister attended, but I don't remember her name. Just that she had so much to say about what Stacy and Terrell didn't do to her liking."

"Wait! What?" Dee said with a shocked expression.

"Yes, honey! She waltzed her size four behind right into that church and immediately began to scrutinize everything from the flowers to the casket. Talking about her brother deserved better. Curtis and Jerome had to help Terrell almost tie Stacy down to keep her from grabbing ol' girl."

"Now where in the world was I?" Dee asked. "That would have been something to see."

"Thankfully, it was before a lot of people had arrived at the church, but you were back in the kitchen with the girls."

"It's probably a good thing," Dee said through clenched teeth. "Because I probably would have laid hands on her."

"Now that's something *I* would have loved to see," Carmen laughed.

"What? I can throw down if I have to," Dee said with a grin.

"Yeah, okay. I hear you, girl."

And they both laughed out loud.

"Enough of that. Where are we going while these folks are gone?" Carmen asked.

"How about Aruba?"

Dee and Carmen both looked over their shoulders to see Stacy walking up.

"Hey, girl," they both said.

"Come grab a seat," Dee motioned as she pulled a chair from under the table. "I hope we weren't being too loud, and you heard us from the driveway."

"No, Nana Jean let me in and told me you were out by the pool," Stacy stated as she poured herself a glass of wine from the bottle of Pinot Noir on the table.

"You know, Aruba does sound nice, but it's going to be crowded with all the vacationers. I was thinking of Italy," Dee said.

"Ooh, now that's a spot I could get down with," Carmen exclaimed.

"Me too," said Stacy.

"Then that settles it. We're going to Italy," Dee yelled.

"You're going where?" Nana Jean asked as she brought them another bottle of wine.

"We are going to Italy the week the girls are at Summer Intensive and the boys are camping."

"Hmm hmm, well, I can't see how any of you think you're going anywhere, and you haven't asked me," Nana Jean said.

"Mom, we are all adults. Why would we need to ask you?" Dee said with a tone.

"Well, for starters," Nana Jean said, "who is going to be the point of contact if something happens to the girls?"

"You, Todd, and Laton, same as always," Carmen retorted.

"How did you figure I wouldn't want to go to Italy?" Nana Jean asked.

"I might find you a new daddy," she said as she whipped her hips from side to side.

The ladies all laughed, and Dee said, "Now, Mom, you know you are more than welcome to go, but every year we've invited you, you've said no."

"Well, I'm not declining this year. Besides, my dear sweet David has been gone for over four years now. I think it's time I start living again," she said. "I believe I still have a little swerve left in me," as she snapped her fingers and walked back inside.

Dee, Carmen, and Stacy all rolled their eyes and laughed until tears started to fall.

"Girl, your mom is truly something serious," Stacy said.

"Baby, there isn't a day that goes by we aren't in full-blown laughter because of her," Dee snorted, still laughing at her mom's antics.

They both quickly stopped laughing as they noticed Carmen sniffling and fighting back tears.

"Ooh no, what's wrong, friend?" Dee asked as Stacy pulled her chair closer to Carmen.

"It's nothing," she said. "I just miss my mom so much, and with everything going on with Gigi Retha… and, and… oh Lord, I just can't," Carmen said before rolling into a full-fledged sob.

"It's okay," they both said to her as Stacy rubbed her back and Dee wiped her tears. "While I know my mom could never take the place of your mom or Gigi Retha, you do know that she looks at you as if you're her own, right?" Dee said.

Carmen sat up and wiped the last of her tears, saying, "Yes," and then immediately began to apologize. "I'm sorry, y'all. I think I may have had too much wine."

"Tuh," Stacy scoffed. "I have never heard of such a thing. Give me that bottle."

They all laughed and continued chatting well into the night.

"What time is it?" Drew growled as Dee slid next to him.

"Umm, 3 a.m. Now go back to sleep."

"Three in the morning, Dee?" Drew switched on the lamp next to his side of the bed and turned to face Dee all in one motion. "What the heck were y'all talking about until 3 a.m.?"

"First off, lower your voice," Dee said sternly. "Secondly, I was at home and Carmen and Stacy live around the corner. Besides, it wasn't like we were out shaking our tails at some club."

"True, but three in the morning?" Drew said again as if he was completely confused.

At this point, Dee sat up in the bed.

"Andrew Demond Gorden!" she exclaimed. "I know full well you don't seriously have an attitude about me sitting out on my damn patio until whatever time I choose."

"Now who needs to lower their voice?" Drew asked.

"It's just not like you, that's all," he replied.

"Oh, it's not like me, but apparently, it is a perfect image of you. Seeing that I recall not two months ago, you, Curtis, and Jerome didn't make it home until after the sun had come up. What was the lie, I mean story again? You all were too intoxicated to drive home from the club, so you all slept in Jerome's truck until you were sober. Yet here I am at home," Dee said as she pulled back the covers and got up, "and you have a problem."

As she pulled on her robe and headed toward the door, Drew asked, "Where are you going?"

"To sleep in the car," Dee snapped and walked out of the room.

"Damn, I messed up," Drew said as he turned off the light and slid back into bed.

The next morning, Drew awakened only to the smell of coffee, which let him know immediately that he was officially in the doghouse. As he walked into the kitchen, he caught a stern eye from Nana Jean, who said, "Good morning," through gritted teeth. That also let him know that she was aware that he was in said doghouse, and she approved the relocation.

"Good morning, ladies," Drew managed to say with a plastered grin on his face. "Is there enough coffee left for me?"

"There should be plenty left," Dee said as she turned her gaze from him to the window. "Trinity is gone to the mall with Keisha and Catrina and should be home around 4 p.m. Laton will be here to watch her until Mom and I get back tomorrow, so you are free to do whatever you had planned."

"I didn't have any plans," Drew said with a sigh. He knew by the fact that she didn't cook breakfast, wouldn't as much as look at him, and had made plans without discussing them with him first, that he may never get a chance to make this up.

"Well, I guess you can just chill out," Dee said.

"What are you and Nana Jean getting into?"

"Nothing. We, well, I just figured today was a good day to just get away and not have to worry about how long I stay," Dee quipped as she brushed past Drew.

"Come on, Dee, that's not fair," Drew turned to follow behind her, but Nana Jean stopped him.

"Son," she said, "Now, I don't generally get in y'all's mess because Lord knows that David and I had our share of run-ins, but you need to just give her time. I don't know what you said, but whatever it was, it hurt her deeply. She'll come around. Just pray."

"Thanks, Nana Jean," Drew said under his breath. He bent down, kissed her on the cheek, and walked out onto the patio.

Chapter 7

Jesus, you're the center of my joy.

"Yes, you better sing!" Nana Jean shouted as she waved her hand. "Hallelujah!" As soon as the choir finished singing, those standing sat down, and the preacher stood up.

"My Lord, my Lord, my Lord!" another person yelled, but Trinity couldn't see. Looking around, she made eye contact with Camille and waved.

"Mom," Trinity whispered as she tapped Dee on the shoulder. "Why are people shouting and waving their hands? And what's wrong with Nana Jean?"

"They are filled with the Holy Spirit, honey. That's all."

"The Holy Spirit," Trinity thought to herself, attempting to make a mental note to research it later.

"Amen. Glory to God!" Bishop Williams said as he walked up to the pulpit. "God is good. Mighty, mighty good, and I'm going to praise Him.

I don't know about you," Bishop Williams said, "but I'm going to praise Him!"

The church erupted with people shouting, "Amen," "Hallelujah," and "Glory!"

Trinity even mouthed, "Yes, Lord," and was shocked to hear her own voice. She immediately looked around to see if anyone had noticed, but they hadn't.

Where did that come from, and why? she thought. *I've never had the urge to say anything before.* Yet today, things felt different, but she wasn't quite sure why. She had this overwhelming feeling of wanting to run and scream all at once.

As Trinity got out of her thoughts, she tuned in just in time to hear Bishop Williams say, "Turn in your Bibles with me to John 4:6-14." Bishop started to read the scripture, and when he finished, he said, "Today's sermon title is 'Thirsty for Living Water.'"

As quickly as Trinity tuned in, she tuned out again. Fully aware of her surroundings but not aware at all. Trinity seemed to be outside of herself.

How is this possible? she thought as she looked down over the entire congregation. *I've got to get back in my body before my mom realizes I'm sitting beside her, dead. I mean, I have to be dead, right? Who just floats up out of their body like this? Who does that?*

While Trinity continued with this battle of sorts, a flicker of light caught her attention, and she followed it. But she was not ready for what she saw.

As soon as she got to the light, what unfolded before her was astonishing, heartbreaking, and scary. *There is no way this is real. It can't be happening. No way!*

"Stop, stop!" she yelled, but none of the people could hear her.

While she continued to look at what was undoubtedly her Uncle Todd being held down by three police officers and several others with guns drawn and pointed at him, she heard a voice.

"Tell your mom what you see."

Trinity looked back over her shoulder and saw the church congregation, focusing on the pew where they were seated. Again, the voice said, "If you want him to survive, tell your mom what you see."

Trinity was overcome with fear and immediately jerked herself out of her trance. Just as she turned to tap her mom on the arm, Dee looked at her and said, "We need to go."

They both immediately jumped up and grabbed their things. As they inched their way out of the pew, Dee whispered something into Drew's ear. He nodded and leaned over to Nana Jean, who did the same. They walked swiftly down the aisle and out the door, instinctively breaking into a run toward the car.

"Mom, Mom!" Trinity panted as they got in the car, and Dee quickly snatched it into gear. "I had an out-of-body experience, and I... I saw."

"Yes, Trinity, I know," Dee interrupted.

But how? Trinity thought, her mind racing. *There is no way she could have known what I saw, what I experienced.* Trinity sat in what could be described as stark silence, but she was actually whispering a prayer only she could hear.

Soon after getting in the car, Dee abruptly brought it to a stop, which felt odd to Trinity. *How in the world does she know where to go? I never told her what I saw or where.*

By the time Trinity got out of the car, Dee was already confronting a police officer, her voice loud and unwavering.

"Tell me what he did!" she demanded. "Why is he in handcuffs, and why is his face bruised?"

The officer only responded, "You can get your answers at the Kirkman Precinct."

As the crowd gathered, distracted by Dee's confrontation, Trinity quietly eased over to the car where Todd was sitting in the back seat.

"Uncle Todd," she whispered.

"Hey, Peanut," Todd replied, attempting a grin, though his swollen face barely allowed it.

"What happened?" she asked.

"Don't you worry about that," he said. "Just know I'm innocent, and I'll be home soon."

"Uncle Todd, they were going to kill you," Trinity said through sniffles.

"Nah, nah," Todd replied. "They just like to rough people up to show they're in charge."

"But I saw—" Trinity trailed off, then quickly changed course. "I saw how they threw you in the car," she said, knowing it wasn't the whole truth. *I'll need to repent before bed tonight,* she thought.

Todd's eyes widened. "Saw what, Peanut?"

"How they threw you in the car," she repeated.

"Listen," Todd said firmly. "I didn't do any of the stuff they're saying, okay? Tell your mom to make them pull the video. I tried to tell them, but they weren't listening."

"Okay, I will," Trinity promised.

"Hey! Get away from that car!"

Trinity jumped when she heard the yelling and saw a police officer running toward her.

"Go!" Todd urged.

Moved by the Whispers

Trinity ran back toward her mom, her heart pounding.

What felt like hours later, Trinity and Dee reconnected with her dad and Nana Jean at the Kirkman Precinct.

"Why are they taking so long to bring him out?" Nana asked, her voice shaky.

"I'm not sure, Mom, but it should be soon," Dee replied. "Let me remind you, they did physically attack him, so he'll be bruised and swollen when you see him."

"Yeah, you told me," Nana snapped, her frustration bubbling over. "I just want these folks to bring my son… my baby, from back there. He isn't some criminal! He's never even jaywalked," she choked out before breaking into sobs again. "Lord, have mercy! Have mercy, dear Lord! Why have they violated my son?"

Trinity sat in silence, still in a state of shock. It wasn't from being at the police precinct, nor from even seeing Todd beaten and swollen. No, she was shocked by two words her mother had spoken earlier: *I know.*

I know? What did she mean by that? How did she know? Trinity silently pondered these questions, watching as Nana Jean paced the floor and her parents busied themselves on their phones.

Eventually, a door swung open, and Uncle Todd emerged.

"Oh my God! No, no, no!" Nana Jean cried out, rushing forward. "What did you do to my baby?" she screamed as she pushed one of the officers.

"Mom, no!" Todd and Dee both yelled, springing into action to put space between Nana Jean and the officer.

As Trinity watched, tears began streaming down her face. Her dad quickly scooped her up and carried her outside.

Drew gently wiped the tears from Trinity's cheeks, but they continued to fall. Her lips moved as she mouthed a word, but no sound came out.

"What is it, Muffin?" Drew asked softly.

Trinity tried again. "Why?" she mouthed, her voice still failing her.

Drew leaned in closer. "Say it again, baby," he urged.

This time, Trinity let out a sound so gut-wrenching, it shook Drew to his core.

"Whyyyyyyy?" she wailed, the cry reverberating through the air.

It was the most raw and painful sound Drew had ever heard and hearing it from his daughter pierced him deeply. All he could do was hold her close as her shoulders shook and her tears soaked through his sleeve.

The more Trinity cried, the angrier Drew became—not because his sleeve was wet, but because he felt powerless. He wanted—no, he *needed*—to do something.

By the time they made it home, Drew was still consumed with anger and frustration. He paced the floor relentlessly, his emotions boiling over.

"Drew, honey, you need to sit down," Dee said gently. "You're going to wear a hole in the bottom of your shoes if you keep this up much longer."

"What am I supposed to do then?" Drew snapped. "You didn't see her face. You didn't hear the distress in her tiny little voice. And you— you didn't..." Drew's voice cracked. As Dee looked up at him, he crumbled to the floor, overwhelmed.

"Oh, Andrew," Dee exclaimed, sliding down to the floor to pull him into her arms. "Babe, it's going to be okay. We've contacted the lawyer, Todd is home, and I've got the names and numbers of several eyewitnesses who were on the scene today. Trinity is going to be okay. I'll schedule an appointment for her to see the therapist tomorrow. It's all going to be okay. Don't beat yourself up, and please don't worry. Matter of fact, let's pray right now."

Andrew looked up at Dee, his red, puffy eyes glistening. A slight smile broke through his pain. "You know, Deloris, this is why I love you. You always manage to stay level-headed, and you always lead us back to God when I'm ready to take another route."

Deloris smiled and let out a soft chuckle. "That's the thug in you."

They both laughed, and then Andrew grabbed Deloris by her hands and began to pray.

The following morning, at breakfast, the atmosphere was still thick with dread and gloom. Everyone ate, but no one spoke, a stark contrast to the usual lively energy of the Gorden household. Silence was typically reserved for nighttime when everyone was asleep—and even then, it wasn't completely quiet because Nana Jean snored like a freight train during her visits.

"Okay, enough of this," Todd declared, slapping his hand on the table with a sudden thud that made Trinity jump.

"Sorry, Peanut, I didn't mean to scare you," Todd said quickly. "Listen, folks, today is a new day, and we are all here right now because God allowed it. So, what we're *not* going to do is walk around here like there's a hole in our sock or we lost our favorite coin. Let's get up and get things shaking."

Todd sprang up from his chair and started shimmying in an exaggerated attempt to do the smooth step.

Trinity burst into a fit of laughter. "Uncle Todd, you're doing it all wrong!"

"Well, show me then!" Todd challenged with a grin.

As though lifted by unseen hands, Trinity rose from her seat and seamlessly transitioned into the dance. "Now *this* is how it's done, Uncle Todd," she said, gliding effortlessly around the table.

"Well, excuse me!" Todd chuckled. "I stand corrected."

The laughter spread around the table, lightening the mood—until the doorbell rang, abruptly cutting the joy short.

Andrew got up and walked toward the front door, and Trinity immediately slid closer to Nana Jean. Another knock came, this one more forceful.

"Just a moment!" Andrew shouted. He mumbled something under his breath as he opened the door but quickly masked it with a surprised, "Hello."

Concerned by his sudden change in tone, Deloris and Todd got up from the table and moved toward the front door. As Trinity stood, Nana Jean motioned firmly for her to sit back down.

"No, ma'am, honey. You get yourself right back in that seat," Nana Jean said.

"But, Nana," Trinity bemoaned.

"But nothing. Sit down. That's grown folks' business, and you are *not* grown."

Trinity plopped back into her chair, folding her arms in frustration. Apparently, she did so a little too forcefully for Nana Jean's liking because she immediately felt the sharp sting of a pinch.

"OUCH!" Trinity yelped.

"Ouch nothing. You better watch yourself, young lady. I don't care how much I love you—I will tighten you up if I have to, and I *mean* it."

"Yes, ma'am," Trinity said, blinking back tears.

Moved by the Whispers

She knew she had crossed the line with Nana Jean. Although Nana had only pinched her three times in her life, each instance was enough to remind her that Nana didn't play around. Trinity had heard enough of Uncle Todd's childhood stories to know that a pinch was the *better* punishment, and she wanted no part of what came next.

"Hello there!" Andrew exclaimed at the door. "We didn't realize you'd be making a house call. Please, come inside."

Trinity heard a deep male's voice reply, "Thank you." She didn't recognize the voice, but its depth made her sit up straighter in curiosity.

"Mr. Bettis, how are you?" a female's voice asked.

Trinity then heard Uncle Todd respond, "In spite of the experience, I'm doing okay."

She didn't recognize the female's voice either, but it was clear that this visit had something to do with the events from the day before.

Just as Trinity tried to settle onto the den sofa to better hear the conversation, Nana Jean turned and said, "Go to your room."

Ugh, Trinity thought. *Nana sure knows how to kill a vibe.* But still smarting from the earlier pinch, she had no desire to risk another or find out what Nana's "next level" discipline entailed.

"Yes, ma'am," Trinity replied quickly, scooting off to her room.

Nana Jean walked into the living room where the others had gathered and apologized for being late.

"As I live and breathe," she said. "Hello, Mrs. Bettis. It has certainly been a long time."

"London and Malachi, you two have definitely grown up!"

"Yes, ma'am, we have," Malachi replied with a laugh.

London and Malachi Glasper were the dynamic brother-sister attorney duo from Glasper & Glasper Law Firm. But to Nana Jean, they were just two kids from the block. The siblings had spent summers in Nashville with their grandparents, Kent and Becky Glasper, who had lived next door to Jean and her husband, David, better known as Nana Jean and Paw Paw Bettis.

"I know Kent and Becky are Godly proud of you two," Nana Jean continued, smiling warmly. "And I want to thank you both so much for taking this case."

"We wouldn't have it any other way," they said in unison.

Chapter 8

"That was the longest eighteen months ever," Todd said. "You're telling me," Nana Jean replied. "I had to sit in that courtroom every day for weeks and listen to the lies they talked about you."

"Well, thanks to Malachi and London, the entire world got to see those cops for what they were—racist and abusing their power," Drew said.

"This was just the first hurdle of this nightmare," Dee added. "There's still the matter of the civil suit."

"It has definitely been long," Trinity chimed in. "You guys missed your trip to Italy, Dad didn't go camping, and I barely made it through my summer dance intensive. When will this be over? Like, seriously, when? My past two summers were ruined outside of dance. I haven't celebrated my birthday in two years! Not to mention I didn't get to go to Camille's birthday party last month. And now, here we are a week away from Thanksgiving. I'm just ready for it to be over."

"We know, baby," Nana Jean said, pulling Trinity close to her. "Peanut, I'm so sorry that this mess has disrupted your life."

"I promise I'll make it up to you," Todd said. "I never imagined something like this happening to me, and I certainly didn't intend for it to affect you." His eyes filled with tears.

"Oh, Uncle Todd, I didn't mean to make you cry," Trinity said as tears welled in her own eyes. She ran to him, and he grabbed her tightly. They both cried, and soon everyone else was crying, too—until Drew decided to break the tension.

He burst into an off-key rendition of *Cry Me a River* by Justin Timberlake. His singing was exactly what they all needed to shift the atmosphere. The tears turned to laughter, filling the room with warmth.

As tradition dictated, the night before Thanksgiving was spent prepping for the big day. Now that Trinity, Camille, Keisha, and Catrina were older, they were part of the tradition, too.

This year, Stacy and Terrell were hosting, so everyone gathered at their house as the day turned to night and the festivities began. The men were all outside, and since Cayden was the only boy, he got to hang with them by default.

This year was different from previous years. Mr. Wayne, Catrina's dad, had passed away from cancer, and Gigi Retha—Camille and Cayden's grandmother—was too weak to stand in the kitchen as she used to. That didn't stop her from running the show, though. Sitting on her stool at the counter, she barked orders alongside Nana Jean, who was as commanding as ever.

Trinity and Camille were tasked with washing and prepping the vegetables, while Catrina and Keisha organized all the seasonings. Dee was at the sink washing the greens, Carmen was whipping sweet potatoes for the pies and soufflé, and Stacy was the unofficial bartender.

Meanwhile, Nana Jean and Gigi Retha were working their magic on the infamous dressing. No one knew the exact recipe, but it was always a hit.

"Hey, Retha," Nana Jean said with a chuckle, "do you remember that year we were at Carmen and Curtis' house for Thanksgiving, when George and David tried to deep fry the turkey?" Nana Jean asked.

"Do I ever! They darn near burned the patio down," Retha replied, laughing.

"Curtis didn't talk to his dad for two days after that," Retha added with a chuckle.

"Oh yes, that was certainly a tense few days," Carmen teased.

"That turkey was charred on the outside and raw on the inside," Dee said, laughing.

"Wait, how do I not remember that?" Stacy asked, confused.

"That was the year you and Terrell took all the kids to Hollywood Studios while we cooked," Nana Jean reminded her.

"So *that's* why we didn't have turkey that year?" Camille asked with a frown.

"Better yet," Keisha said, "that explains why your mom's awning was drooping!"

Catrina and Trinity burst into laughter, dramatically reenacting how the awning had sagged.

Everyone laughed along as they eased back into their work, and time passed smoothly in the warm and lively kitchen.

Meanwhile, the guys were outside "telling lies," according to Gigi Retha. But as long as the turkey, ribs, and ham turned out right, no one truly cared.

"Hey, Dad!" Cayden called out. "Watch this."

Cayden proceeded to perform a *Tobikomizuki Nihon, Gyakuzuki, Mawashigeri, Ushirogeri, Uraken, Gyakuzuki* combination. Drew and Todd cheered in amazement.

"Man, Cayden is smooth with the karate moves," Todd said.

"Yes, he is," Curtis replied. "He loves it and soaks it up like a sponge. He's already earned a black belt for his age range."

"What?" Drew exclaimed. "Dude, didn't you guys put him in karate like yesterday?"

"He's been taking classes for eight months now. His Sensei says he's his top student and has caught on faster than any kid he's taught in the past 10 years," Curtis explained.

"That's dope," Todd said. "Hey, Cayden, do you think you can teach me some of those moves?"

"Well, I can try," Cayden replied. "The question is, are you going to be able to do them? I mean, you're a little bit older and a lot stiffer than I am."

They all laughed as Todd looked at Curtis with a *What the heck?* expression.

"Let me show you something," Todd said, proceeding to complete a full standing backflip with a twist into a back tuck.

"Hey now, we aren't going to the emergency room," Drew joked.

"Wait a minute!" Cayden screamed. "How did I not know you knew how to do that? Like, what other Jedi secrets are you withholding, Uncle Todd?"

"Aww, little man, no secrets. I just had to show you I'm not old."

"Where did you learn that?" Cayden asked, beyond amazed at the tumbling combination and eager for answers. "Please teach me. Like, seriously, teach me," Cayden pleaded.

"Slow down, grasshopper. One thing at a time," Todd said. "You teach me your karate moves, and I'll teach you my gymnastics moves."

"Gymnastics? Isn't that for girls?" Cayden asked.

"Nah, man," Todd replied. "Come over here and let me show you something."

The two walked toward the TV in the covered patio area.

"Todd is about to cost me some money," Curtis said to Drew. "I can feel my wallet getting lighter as I speak."

"Ha, I bet you can," Drew replied. "I'd love to have a son. Not saying Trinity isn't the light of my life—because she is—but it's just different with a son, you know."

"It isn't too late. I mean, Trinity is only twelve," Curtis said.

"Not too late?" Drew sucked in his breath. "It's not even the fact that she's twelve. It's the convincing Dee part that has us stranded at sea. There are days I feel like she's leaning toward having another baby—or heck, even adopting—and just as quickly as I feel like I see the shoreline, she's back out in the deep."

"That has to be hard," Curtis said. "What do you think is causing her to hesitate?"

"If only I knew," Drew replied, flipping a slab of ribs on the grill. "I feel like it has something to do with her childhood, and it's something she's not willing to talk about. I mean, Trinity was a pleasant surprise because, if I'm honest, I don't think Dee ever meant for us to have kids at all."

"Now, Drew," Curtis scolded, "there's no way Dee didn't want kids. Have you seen your wife with your daughter? You can't seriously tell me that you've ever thought she didn't want her."

"Yeah, I see all of that," Drew said, "but I know what I know."

The two men simultaneously took swigs of their sodas, exchanged an unspoken look of understanding, and shifted the conversation to something more pleasant.

But Curtis made a mental note to talk with Carmen later—this had him concerned for his friend.

"Everyone, please listen up," Dee commanded. "We have exactly two hours to get showered and changed before the photographer arrives for our annual Thanksgiving and Christmas pictures."

Dee was barking orders like a drill sergeant, but there was no way she was going to let this go off as anything other than stellar. "Ladies, you'll use the bathrooms on the main level; guys, you have the basement and pool house bathrooms. Understood?"

"Yes," everyone responded, then peeled off to get themselves together.

The annual photoshoot had become a tradition long before Trinity and Camille were born. It started as a way for the group to let their parents know they were okay when they didn't return home for the holidays while in college. When Drew and Curtis began their master's programs at MIT, that's where they met Terrell. Somehow, they all ended up in Florida, and the friendship flourished, adding Jerome and Wayne to the mix.

Fast forward a few years, Drew asked Dee to marry him. According to Curtis, it was because Dee was about to break up with him, feeling that Drew was dragging his feet. They had been together for six years, starting as freshmen at Hampton. They split for a minute when Drew went to MIT and Dee went to New York School of Interior Design because Drew felt that Dee wasn't giving him the support he needed—despite the fact that she wasn't exactly in an easy program herself. Thank the Lord for meddlesome friends and family who knew Dee was exactly what Drew needed in his life and didn't stop until those two were back together. As they say, the rest was history.

Curtis snapped back from his thoughts and found himself alone at the grill.

"Drew!" Curtis called. "How you just leave me, man?"

Drew yelled from the pool house that he'd told Curtis to come on and get dressed. Curtis shook his head and walked toward the pool house to dress with the rest of the gang.

As everyone gathered around the pool to begin taking the first of many pictures, the photographer directed everyone where to stand. Cayden was sitting at the pool's edge, with Trinity and Camille to his left, and Keisha and Catrina to his right. Camille and Keisha had their hands on Cayden's shoulders, while Trinity and Catrina were in a one-knee kneeling position. Behind them were Nana Jean and Gigi Retha, sitting on stools, with all the parents interspersed around and behind the kids.

"This is royal," Keisha said.

"I know, right?" Camille responded. "I feel like we are princes and princesses of some utopian country, like Zumunda, from the movie *Coming to America*."

They both laughed, and Nana Jean and Gigi Retha began to explain that they should always feel like royalty because they came from kings and queens from real tribes in Africa.

"Are you for real, Nana Jean?" Trinity asked, her eyes bright and full of excitement.

"Yes, dear, I am. I'll tell you more after these pictures."

"Cool," Catrina responded.

"Very cool," Cayden echoed. "I've never really liked history, but I think this is about to be epic."

"Epic indeed," Stacy and Todd said at the same time.

As soon as the pictures were over, the kids ran to their grandmothers, eager to hear more about how they came from royalty.

"Go change your clothes," Terrell and Carmen both said.

"Yes, go get out of those clothes right now before you get them dirty," Dee responded.

"Yes, ma'am. Yes, sir," each of the kids replied as they scattered to get dressed.

"You two know these kids are not going to let you rest," Drew said to Jean and Retha.

They both laughed. Retha said, "Oh baby, trust me, I'm going to get my rest in good fashion. These kids are not going to wear me out. Heck, I'm tired now just watching all that energy they have."

Jean responded, "Honey, ain't that the truth. Those girls flit, spin, and roll around this house all day. And that little Cayden, does he ever sleep?"

"Yes, ma'am, I do," Cayden said.

Nana Jean laughed as she looked around to see his cute little round face standing in the doorway. "Come here," she commanded. "Have you hugged me today?"

Cayden came over and wrapped his arms around Nana Jean, squeezing as tightly as he could. She looked down at him and told him that she loved him and thought she saw a hint of a mustache appearing.

"Whoa! Did you hear that, Gigi? Nana said I'm getting a mustache!" Cayden exclaimed.

"Let me see," Gigi said.

Cayden hopped over to her, and she took his face in her hand, turning it from side to side and tilting it up and down. She looked over at Jean and winked with a sly smile, to which Jean responded in kind.

"Well, you know," Retha said, "I think I see a hair or two coming through."

"Listen, you can't go telling everyone because that will make it stop growing," Gigi Retha told him.

"Yes, and you can't stare into the mirror either," Nana Jean added.

"Okay, okay," Cayden said with a smile. "Man, this is the best day ever. I'm from royalty, and I'm getting a mustache," he said as he ran out of the room to get the girls.

"Now Jean, why did you lie to that boy?" Retha asked.

"I'm just boosting his self-esteem," Jean replied. "He certainly doesn't need one of those little girls at his school telling him first. His head will be way too big, and we won't be able to deal with him."

They both chuckled and high-fived each other just as the kids came back into the family room.

"Come on, Nana and Gigi, we're ready to hear our story of royalty," they said eagerly.

"Okay, calm down," they said. "Dee, Carmen, Stacy, y'all come on," Jean called.

A faint "Yes, ma'am" could be heard from the kitchen, and soon, they all appeared with Drew, Curtis, and Todd in tow.

"Is everyone settled?" Retha asked.

"Yes!" the kids yelled.

"Let's get started then," Nana Jean stated. "Well, Retha and I have been conducting research regarding our family lineage for some time. We started before either of your grandfathers passed away."

"Paw Paw David and Papa George," Cayden said.

"Yes," Nana responded. "They both died before you were born, but you look just like your Papa George. Now, back to the story."

Retha jumped in and added, "We completed DNA23 and 23Ancestry, but our best results came from AllAfricanAncestry.com because it was able to tell us exactly which tribe we originated from."

There were multiple "Wow's," "Oh my God's," and "Are you for real?" heard across the room.

"Listen, listen," Jean said. "What I'm about to say next is important. Knowing where you originated from is a critical component to knowing who you are. It's more than just knowing who your parents or grandparents are. It's a sense of pride, a greater sense of belonging that was stripped away from us so many years ago. A stripping away that has left us longing."

"The results were able to tell us our specific African country and tribe of origin," Retha continued. "Luckily for you, we have the information for us as your mothers and for your fathers as well."

Dee and Carmen looked at one another in shock.

"So let me get this straight," Andrew stated. "You know exactly what tribe and country you originated from based on a single test?"

"That's what we're saying," Retha and Jean responded in unison.

"Oh man, I need to try this for myself," Drew replied.

"Well, you'd be happy to know that we have the results for each of you," Jean beamed.

"How?" Drew, Curtis, Stacy, and Terrell questioned.

"Well, Stacy, when your mother, Margaret, took ill back in 2007, we all had the discussion that we wanted to know where we came from and to provide that information to each of you," Jean explained. "We immediately got to work ordering the kits, but we didn't send them off for results right away due to Margaret's passing. However, it was your mom who decided that, whatever the results, we would wait to tell you until the girls were old enough to appreciate the information."

"As you know," Retha began, "just weeks after Margaret passed, we lost Drew's parents, Dorothy and Fletcher, to a drunk driver, so that put a pause on things. In 2009, your dad, Clarence, passed that May, and Terrell's mom, Adrienne, died in October."

"And it just seemed all downhill after that," Jean expounded. "We lost David, George, and Lloyd all in 2010. That left Retha and me trying to pull this all together without you knowing. And then..." Jean began but stopped as her eyes filled with tears.

"Oh Nana, don't cry," Trinity said.

"Lord, help me," Jean exclaimed. She drew in a breath and began again. "After Retha was diagnosed with cancer in 2012, I'd lost all hope that this would ever happen. My friend was so sick, and the doctors had all but given up. But she recovered, and we were back in stride again. But that darn cancer came back, and it has been wreaking havoc and raising hell for over a year now, and..."

"And we decided," Retha jumped in, "that it was now or never. So let's get this party started. Do you guys and dolls want to know the results?"

"Yes!" everyone said, through teary eyes.

"Drew's maternal and Terrell's paternal lines come from the Bubi People of Bioko Island. There's a possibility you are cousins," Jean began.

"Carmen, Stacy, and Dee, each of your maternal lines come from Nigeria, with Carmen being from the Hausa tribe, and Stacy and Dee being of mixed Hausa-Fulani origin."

"Curtis, your paternal line is from The Gambia, and your tribe is the Mandinka people."

"Drew, yours and Carmen's paternal lines are from the Igbo people of Nigeria and Cameroon."

"Terrell, your maternal line originates from the Dogon tribe in Mali."

"Stacy, your paternal line hails from the Maasai tribe in Kenya."

"And Dee, your paternal line is derived from the Nigerian Yoruba tribe."

"There is so much more to know and understand," Jean added, "but we will reveal all of that later on over this weekend. Let's just bask in the knowledge of who we are. Can we do that?" Jean and Retha asked.

"Yes!" Everyone responded excitedly as they each chirped about this newfound information.

The following day was Thanksgiving, and the house was alive with an abundance of noise. As was tradition, everyone spent the night at the host house. Jean and Retha were sitting out on the screened patio, sipping coffee and talking, when Stacy opened the door.

"Good morning, ladies!" she said.

"Good morning, baby," they both replied.

"Are they ready for breakfast?" Jean asked.

"Oh, Dee made everyone eat cereal," Stacy laughed. "She said we weren't going to run her mom into the ground."

"That sounds just like that child," Jean said with a tsk.

"Sure does, because it sounds just like you," Retha replied with a laugh.

They looked at one another and burst into a full-on belly laugh because they both knew it was the truth. Stacy just smiled and said that Dee was ready when they were to prepare the final items for dinner, then slid back into the house, leaving them to spend their time together.

Sometime later, the table was set, and they gathered with thankful hearts.

"Wow! What a spread this is," Cayden exclaimed. "I don't think we've ever had this much food for any holiday."

"This is definitely one for the ages," Todd agreed.

"It is indeed, but we have so much to be thankful for this year," Jean responded. "You being cleared of those heinous charges, Retha being healed from cancer, Drew's business expanding—just so much to be thankful for."

"Lord, I thank You," Jean said, her hands raised and tears streaming down her face.

As she openly gave God praise, everyone else joined in with their own form of praise. Trinity, Camille, and Keisha began to sing, and a full-on worship service of Thanksgiving was had by all.

Chapter 9

"I can't believe the holidays are over, and we go back to school on Monday," Trinity groaned to Camille over the phone.

"Me either," Camille agreed. "But on the bright side, at least you get to see Kingston," she added in a sing-song voice.

"I sure do—right along with you seeing Elias and Keisha seeing Sullivan," Trinity responded.

"Wow! Who would have thought that we would all have boyfriends?"

"Well, not all of us," Camille pointed out. "Catrina is still giving Reggie a hard time."

"Yeah, and I totally don't get why," Trinity said. "Hey, let's call Keisha and see if she knows what's up since they live together. Maybe she's only being tight-lipped with us."

"I'll conference her in," Camille said, putting Trinity on hold. A short moment later, she returned with both Keisha and Catrina on the line.

"Hey, Trinity, girl," they both said as soon as Camille called her name.

"Hey, y'all. What's up?" Trinity asked.

"What's up," Keisha bemoaned, "is that school starts Monday, which means we only have two weeks until the winter formal."

"Girl!" Camille shouted. "How did I totally forget about that? I have absolutely nothing to wear, and I need to make sure Elias, and I are on point."

They all groaned at Camille, who was always being extra.

"No. What's up is that we all have dates except Catrina," Trinity stated. "And I, for the record, am not going stag just because she won't give Reggie the time of day."

"Wait a minute!" Catrina shouted. "I never asked you guys to go to the spring sneaker ball alone. You guys decided that on your own, so don't blame me."

"Catrina, do we look like a bunch of Fairweather friends to you?" Trinity asked. "FGFL, right?"

Catrina said nothing.

"Umm, FGFL, right?" Trinity repeated herself with a hint of attitude.

"Yeah, girl. FGFL," Catrina said, barely above a whisper.

Keisha immediately asked her what was wrong because tears were streaming down her face.

"Hey, y'all, Catrina is crying," Keisha said.

Trinity and Camille both said almost simultaneously, "We'll be right over," and hung up the phone.

A short time later, all the girls were nestled together on the sofa in Keisha's parents' entertainment room. Catrina had managed to stop crying by the time Camille and Trinity arrived, but she was still visibly upset and unusually quiet.

Keisha got up, locked the door to the room, and turned around with her hands on her hips.

"Alright, what's going on with you, Catrina?" she demanded.

"It's nothing," Catrina said, her eyes starting to water again.

"It can't be nothing," Trinity said. "You started tearing up before Keisha even finished the question."

"Like, seriously, Catrina," Camille crooned as she rubbed her back. "What's the deal?"

Before Catrina could respond, Trinity had a vision—and it wasn't good. She saw Reggie and Catrina at his place, standing near the pool house, talking. Then Reggie's father appeared, screaming, but Trinity couldn't tell whom. Just as she was coming out of the vision, Catrina started to speak.

"Okay, so listen," Catrina said. "What I'm about to tell you, can't leave this room. You can't say anything to anyone, and you can't treat Reggie any differently. Got it?"

"Got it," they each responded.

Catrina placed her right hand out with her palm up, a signal they all recognized as the cue to make the FGFL pledge. Each of them placed their right hand on top of the previous girl's and repeated together:

"We rise, we fall, but together, we stand tall. No matter near or far, we'll always answer the call. I am not my sister's keeper; I am my sister. Friend Girls For Life."

After the pledge, they hugged one another and sat in a circle on the floor. They all knew that if the pledge card was pulled, it meant things were serious.

"So, I know you guys have been pushing me to date Reggie for the last year," Catrina began. "Here's the thing—and please don't be angry—we have been secretly dating this entire time."

"WHAT?!" the other three screamed in unison.

"How could you not tell us? And by us, I mean especially me," Keisha asked. "I mean, we *do* live in the same house together."

"Because I—we—couldn't risk anyone finding out. Especially his parents," Catrina explained.

"I'm confused," Camille said. "What would be so bad about everyone knowing?"

"As you all know, Reggie is biracial."

"Duh! We know," Trinity said, rolling her eyes. "So, what does that have to do with—" She stopped talking abruptly as a voice echoed in her mind: *"His parents don't approve."*

"What were you going to say, Trinity?" Camille asked, nudging her.

"It doesn't matter. Let Catrina finish her story."

"It has everything to do with it," Catrina continued, "because Reggie's parents want him to only date white girls. His father says Black girls are problematic and too independent. He claims that if Reggie dates a white girl, she'll be more submissive and gentler, and his mother agrees."

"Now hold up one minute," Keisha said with a whole lot of attitudes. "So, you mean to tell me that you and Reggie have to hide your relationship because his parents are mega buttholes?"

"Basically, yes. That's exactly what I'm saying," Catrina admitted with a sigh. "Reggie doesn't want to date white girls. He said he's tried it, and it doesn't feel right. He feels like he's on a deserted island. It's awful because all we want to do is be together, but we can't."

Catrina paused for a moment, then continued. "His father caught me at their house last week and went off on me. We tried to tell him we were just studying—which we were, because we had a pre-calculus test the next day—but he wasn't buying it. He accused me of trying to weasel my way into Reggie's life to take him down. He said Reggie was going to make something of himself and that he wouldn't let a 'fast-tail, low-life, no-ambition-having hoochie' ruin his son's chances of making it to the NFL."

Catrina took a shaky breath before adding, "Then he told me to leave and said that if he or his wife caught me talking to Reggie again, they'd have me charged with harassment."

As soon as Catrina finished, she realized she had been holding her breath. She gasped and then melted into tears. "I don't know what to do, but I'm miserable not talking to him. We have no idea who might be watching, so we pass notes in class by dropping them into each other's lockers."

"Why haven't you told Mom and Dad?" Keisha asked. "I mean, I know damn well—oops, sorry y'all. We vowed never to curse, but this has me heated. I know for certain that neither of them would stand for you being treated like this if they knew."

"I know," Catrina sighed, "but Reggie's dad is the District Attorney. How are Momma Stacy and Daddy T going to wrestle against that? That man knows people in some pretty high places. Not to mention that Reggie's mom sits on, I swear, practically every board committee in this city."

"Valid point," Camille agreed, "but shouldn't we at least see what they could do?"

"Catrina's unfortunately right," Trinity chimed in. "There's nothing that can be done from an individual or personal standpoint, but if we take it to God in prayer, He has the power to change anything."

They all agreed and joined hands to pray that God would change the hearts of Reggie's parents, give Reggie and Catrina the strength to stand against the odds, help them be supportive friends, and expose Reggie's parents for their bigotry. The last part of the prayer was from Keisha, who was still very upset by what she'd just learned.

"Let's agree to pray every day at 8:00 am for the next week."

"Agreed," they all said, hugging one last time before Camille chimed in, "I'm hungry."

"Nothing new about that," Keisha commented. They all laughed and headed out of the room and down the stairs to the kitchen.

Two weeks later, the girls were in Camille's room preparing for the winter formal.

"Hey guys, I just wanted to say thanks for coming up with a plan for Reggie and me to be together at the dance."

"Don't sweat it," Trinity said. "That's what FGFL is all about."

"I have to admit the plan was definitely a clutch move on Trinity's part," Keisha added. "I had totally forgotten about Hannah Claire from our days in Girl Scout Troop #197."

"Yeah," Trinity said, "she and I still see each other during our piano recitals and competitions. I just called her up and asked if she wanted to hang with a group of us, and she said sure. Then Camille had Elias ask Ian if he wanted to hang out since he's new to the school and doesn't really know anyone. So, we introduced him to Hannah Claire and suggested they go as a couple, knowing it was just a cover for the pictures. Don't forget, you'll be to Reggie's right and Hannah Claire to his left. All of you will be wearing similar colors so it looks more like a coincidence than intentional. We'll all dance in a cluster so it won't seem like you and Reggie are together, even though you are."

"What about slow dances?" Catrina inquired.

"We have that covered," Camille said. "We'll round-robin with each other's dates. Again, no one will be the wiser, and we'll make sure you and Reggie get time together."

"You three really are the best friends and sisters a girl could ever have."

"FGFL!" Camille shouted through cupped hands to make her voice seem deeper.

"FGFL!" they all repeated through giggles and smiles as they finished dressing for the dance. But deep down, Trinity knew everything wasn't going to go as planned.

At the dance, the group gathered around a table in the corner, laughing, talking, and snapping pictures with their phones. As soon as they heard, "Put your pinky rings up to the moon," they all jumped up and headed to the dance floor.

"I love this song," Reggie said to no one in particular.

Catrina heard him and replied, "Yeah, I know. It's mine, too," as she continued to shimmy and shake to the beat of the music.

They danced until the song ended and transitioned into a slow song. Hannah Claire winked at Catrina, giving her the go-ahead to dance with Reggie as she grabbed Ian's hand and placed it around her waist. Trinity and Kingston coupled up, as did Sullivan and Keisha, while Camille and Elias headed to the drink table.

As the song continued, Trinity had a weird feeling wash over her— one she was all too familiar with. She attempted to end the dance, but Kingston held her tighter and whispered in her ear that he wasn't ready to let her go. She continued to dance, her breath weighted with anticipation of the premonition she knew was coming.

The doors burst open, and ***pop, pop, pop,*** echoed through the room, followed by screams. Trinity froze, her eyes darting around the chaos until they landed on Catrina, crumpled on the dance floor a few feet away. Her pink dress was turning a deep burgundy as blood pooled around her. Desperation filled Trinity's eyes as she pulled away from Kingston.

"What did I do wrong?" he asked, confused.

"Nothing," she replied quickly, "but we've got to get out of here before it's too late."

Uncertain but trusting her, Kingston nodded and hurried to tell Keisha and Elias what Trinity had said. By the time they regrouped near Trinity, Reggie, Catrina, Ian, and Hannah Claire, the doors burst open again.

"Duck!" Trinity yelled as the shots started blasting across the room.

They huddled on the floor, trembling. Ian spotted an opportunity to escape and urged them to follow him. Keisha, paralyzed with fear, hesitated.

"Come on, Keisha!" they pleaded. "We can't stay here!"

Slowly inching across the floor, Camille slipped, quickly catching herself. She assumed she had stepped in fruit punch near the drink table. But as soon as they reached the back hallway leading to the Science building, she realized it was blood. Camille started to scream, but Elias clamped his hand over her mouth.

"We have to stay quiet," he whispered urgently. "The shooter could still be in the building."

They exchanged wide-eyed glances, each in a state of shock. Only then did they realize they were covered in their friends' blood. Whose, they couldn't be sure.

The guys handed their coats to the girls, and they began making their way through the dark corridor toward the Science building. The screams grew fainter behind them, but the sound of sirens grew louder as police and ambulances arrived.

Once inside the Science building, they tried each classroom door, only to find each locked.

"Wait," Sullivan said suddenly. "Mr. Jones never locks his door. Let's go there!"

Sullivan and Elias led the way, with Ian, Reggie, and Kingston pulling up the rear. The girls stayed in the middle, huddled together. As they rounded the corner toward Mr. Jones' room, gunshots rang out again, sounding terrifyingly close.

Hannah Claire gasped, clutching Camille tightly.

"Be quiet!" Trinity hissed. "The shots are behind us. If we're going to survive this night, we have to move now!"

Elias reached Mr. Jones' door and checked the handle. It opened. He motioned for everyone to follow, and they quickly slipped inside. Kingston and Sullivan shoved a desk in front of the door and locked it. They all moved to the back of the room just as new shots echoed through the halls.

"Are we going to live to tell this story?" Catrina asked through tears.

Ian tried to reassure them. "We are. We'll make it out of this."

But Trinity wasn't so sure.

"If you guys believe in God," she said, her voice trembling as a single tear rolled down her cheek, "now would be the perfect time to pray. And I mean sincerely pray."

Chapter 10

"*Tonight, on WFTV 9 News.*" Trinity and Camille were sitting at the dining room table as the news reporter began her ritualistic monologue. For the most part, they had her tuned out, but as soon as they each heard, *"We will be talking to experts about the lingering effects of the school shooting that happened one year ago today,"* Camille grabbed the remote and turned off the TV.

"Ugh, JESUS! Why are they still talking about this?" Camille whined.

Trinity replied in her head, but nothing came out of her mouth.

"Trin," Camille said, nudging her. "Did you hear what I asked?"

"Yeah, I answered you."

"No, you didn't," Camille quipped. "You're just sitting there, staring off into space. What is it you aren't telling me—or anyone, for that matter—about that night? Did you have a premonition?"

Trinity didn't respond.

"Come on, Trin, we're friends—best friends, in fact."

Trinity lowered her head and took a deep breath before looking up and meeting Camille's questioning eyes.

"FGFL, right?" she said.

"Yes, FGFL," Camille responded, holding out her hand, palm up—their sign of truth and solidarity.

"I saw the premonition just before it happened. That's how I was able to warn everyone in the group, but I couldn't save everyone."

"Well, you warned more than just us. Amber Carpenter said she and Marvin McCain survived because they saw us duck down just before the shooting started. They followed us out the side door of the gym but turned another way once they got outside."

"I suppose that's a good thing," Trinity said sullenly.

"You suppose? Girl, you're like a modern-day time traveler or something! I assure you… you saved way more lives than you think."

"Maybe so," Trinity said, "but I ruined some, too."

"How?" Camille asked.

"I honestly can't answer that, but I feel completely at fault. That's why my mom has me in therapy."

"Trinity, we're all in therapy. Reggie is suffering more than anyone. His parents are missing, and he had to change schools to live with his aunt. At least now, he can openly date Catrina."

Trinity just shrugged, got up from the table, and walked into the kitchen. Camille followed her, and they each made a snack. Just as they were about to sit down, Cayden rushed through the door.

"Did you hear the news?"

"What news?" they both asked.

"They found Reggie's parents."

"Seriously?"

"Yeah, seriously," Cayden replied before running off to his room.

Camille and Trinity went into the living room and turned on the TV, hoping to find something related to what they'd just heard. Just as they settled on a news station, Camille's mom called from the kitchen.

"Girls, could you come here, please?"

"Ugh," they both groaned under their breath, but they responded in unison, "Yes, ma'am."

As they rounded the corner into the kitchen, they saw both their moms standing there with weary, strained expressions.

"Have a seat," Carmen instructed, and both girls sat down. Dee began talking, but Trinity only caught the words, "The police have found Reggie's parents, and they are both deceased from an apparent murder-suicide."

Camille sobbed into her hands, but Trinity sat stoically, replaying the words in her head: deceased, murder, suicide, guns used in the school shooting, unclear motive. Without hesitation, she spoke six words.

"They were trying to kill Catrina."

As soon as she said it, she got up and walked to the door. Looking over her shoulder at her mom, Mrs. Smith, and Camille, who stood staring in shock, she simply walked out. There was no way she could tell them that she had called in the tip to the hotline about where to find their bodies—because she'd had a vision the night before. She couldn't tell anyone, but she knew soon, everyone would know.

As if the past year hadn't been awful enough, entering the school on Monday after the news of Reggie's parents was the worst of the worst. Chatter filled the hallways. Teachers were talking, students were talking, and news reporters were all over the front lawn. Trinity was thankful that Reggie had changed schools, hoping he wasn't dealing with the same drama. But she knew he was.

He and Catrina had hung out with Trinity and Kingston on Saturday, and he talked about how it seemed to never end. Reporters constantly called his aunt or showed up at their house or school. He mentioned he was in the process of changing his last name from Johnson to Turner, his grandmother's maiden name, to distance himself from the chaos.

Kingston had asked him if he had any idea why his parents did what they did. Reggie simply replied, "Because of hatred."

He then shared what a day in his home life had been like. Reggie explained that, although his father was Black, he was very fair-skinned and assimilated as a white man. He hated everything Black—especially Reggie's mother.

"In fact, he married my mom because he knew his own mother wouldn't approve. That hatred ran our home. There was no love—only expectations. I was expected to act like a white boy. I was supposed to say I was half Italian if anyone asked about my skin tone. And I was only allowed to date white girls."

Meeting and liking Catrina was a major no. Reggie revealed that the reason he missed the entire basketball season last year was because his father dislocated his shoulder when he refused to agree to cut contact with Catrina.

Kingston was in utter shock. "Dude, we're best friends. How could you not tell me what was going on with you?"

"What was I supposed to say?" Reggie asked. "That my dad was Black but passing as white? That he and my mom hated Black people? How was I supposed to say that with a straight face and still have us remain friends?"

"I don't know," Kingston said, running his hand over his head. "But I feel like I wasn't a very good friend because I had no clue."

"That's how it needed to be," Reggie responded. "Look, I don't hold any of you responsible for what I endured at the hands of my parents. Just know that I didn't then, and I don't now or agree with their beliefs. And I'm going to need you all now like I've never needed you before. This stuff is heavy, and I feel like I'm going to break," Reggie said, tears welling in his eyes. "It's hard to walk around with your head held high when people whisper about you every day. They point and stare, assuming they know the whole story when they actually don't. I hear my aunt cry herself to sleep every night because this is taking such a toll on her. I'm just grateful she doesn't have any kids that would be affected by this quagmire my parents left behind."

Kingston walked over to Reggie and put his hand on his shoulder. "We've got you, dude, day or night. Don't you forget it."

"I won't," Reggie said. Then he shrugged Kingston off and jokingly asked, "Has anyone ever told you that you're very heavy-handed?"

They both laughed, embraced one another, and headed outside to the pool.

As Trinity brought herself back to the present, the timing was perfect, as Mrs. Doss, her French teacher, was asking her a question. "Comment te sens-tu aujourd'hui, Trinité?"

Trinity responded, "Je suis absolument fabuleux."

"Très bien," said Mrs. Doss as she moved across the room. Everything she said was in French, so you had to be on your A-game. She wasn't one for excuses of any kind.

"Demain, il y aura un quiz, alors assurez-vous d'étudier les chapitres 6 et 7," she announced.

"Ugh," everyone moaned, knowing the quiz would be difficult.

"Chut. Aucune plainte. Étudiez," she snapped.

"Madame Doss, combien de questions y aura-t-il dans le quiz?" Jill asked.

Trinity rolled her eyes. Jill was the type who made straight A's without even trying. Did it even matter how many questions were on the quiz? Just as Mrs. Doss was preparing to answer, the bell rang, signaling the end of class.

As soon as Trinity entered the hallway, she saw Camille. "Hey, girl, hey," she said.

"Hey, girl, how was French class?"

"Honey, the usual. Hard. Mrs. Doss is giving a quiz tomorrow, so be prepared when you get in there today."

"Bet," Camille said as she started into the classroom. "Yo Trinity, we still on for tonight?"

"You bet. Are Keisha and Catrina coming?"

"I believe so, but I'll check with Keisha when she gets in class."

"Sounds good. See you after class at our usual spot."

"See you," Camille said, turning to enter Mrs. Doss's class.

Trinity and the rest of the gang met up as usual in their regular spot and waited for their buses. Elias and Kingston rode a different bus than everyone else. Even though they all lived in Lake Nona, Elias and Kingston didn't live in Lake Nona Golf and Country Club. They lived in Summerdale Park. Although it was only about six streets over from where Sullivan and Camille lived, it required a different bus.

Their bus was always the first to arrive, so as soon as they left, the rest of us soon followed. "Meeting at my house at six to study for the French test," Elias said as he stepped onto the bus. Everyone agreed as Elias disappeared, and the bus pulled away.

Our bus pulled up next, and we went to our usual seats, chatting about the day until we reached our stops, knowing we'd all see each other again in a few hours.

Chapter 11

"Hey, Peanut, how are you?" Todd asked as Trinity walked into the house. "Uncle Todd, aren't you a sight for sore eyes," Trinity replied.

Todd laughed and put her in a headlock. "You've been hanging around your grandmother too much, I see."

Trinity poked Todd in the side, knowing he was ticklish and would let her go. As she fixed her hair, she asked, "Where is everyone?"

"Outside on the patio," Todd said. "Your dad is grilling tonight."

"Oh yeah," Trinity said with a grin, rubbing her hands together. She dropped her book bag on the floor next to the island and walked outside.

"There's my Muffin," Drew said as soon as Trinity appeared on the patio.

"Hey, Dad," she replied with a smile. She walked over to give him a hug.

Her mom asked, "How did the study session go?"

"It went well," Trinity said, "but I'm not sure if it went well enough. Mrs. Doss has really been serving it to us lately. It seems like no matter how much you study, it's never quite enough. She always throws in something you didn't see or hear in class."

"Well, it sounds like you have some more studying to do," Dee responded.

"She most definitely does," chimed Nana Jean. "We don't half-do anything around here. Excellence, and nothing less, young lady."

"Yes, ma'am," Trinity sighed, all the while thinking to herself, *This is the time I need a premonition so I can see the answers on this test.* Quickly jumping back to the present, she asked, "What's for dinner? I'm starving."

Drew ran down the list: "Chicken, steaks, baked potatoes, and grilled veggies will be coming in hot to a table near you in about five minutes."

"Dad," Trinity laughed, "stop trying to sound like a used car salesman. It's not your thing."

Everyone laughed, except Drew. "Now, Muffin, don't do your old man like that. I think I could be a pretty good used car salesman if needed."

"Yeah, okay," Trinity said before walking back inside to wash up for dinner.

"Baby, dinner was perfect," Dee said to Drew.

"Yes, it was," everyone confirmed.

"I'll get the dishes," Trinity said as she got up from the table.

"Oh no, you will not," said Nana Jean. "You have some studying to do. Excellence, remember?"

"Yes, ma'am," Trinity chuckled.

"Todd and I will clean the kitchen," Nana Jean added.

"I was about to head out," Todd exclaimed.

"I know," she said, "just like you always do and always have. First to sit down to eat, last to help clean up. But you're cleaning tonight, son, so let's go."

"Yes, ma'am," Todd huffed.

"Oh, don't think you're too grown to be dealt with, son," Nana Jean said firmly. "I'm your mother, and I'll tell you what to do until my dying breath."

"All I said was yes, ma'am!" Todd exclaimed, shrugging his shoulders at Dee with a pleading look for help.

"I didn't like your tone when you said it," Nana Jean replied. "Now, come on and let's clean up this kitchen so you can get to wherever you're trying to go."

"He's probably going over to Laton's," Trinity said in a sing-song voice. "Todd and Laton, sitting in a tree..."

"Hey, hey now," Dee interrupted. "Enough of that. Leave my little brother alone. It's okay if he likes Laton. I wouldn't mind if they ended up a couple."

"I don't know if I like it, though," Drew said. "That's my little cousin, and I've seen how Todd gets down—if you know what I mean."

"Really, dude?" Todd said, giving Drew a look.

"Sorry, man, but you know you like to love them and leave them."

"Man, that's the old me. I'm serious about Laton. She pushes me to do better, be better, and want more out of life than just random, meaningless sex."

"Whoa, dude!" Drew exclaimed. "I know you aren't sexing my cousin, are you?"

"No, man, calm down. Laton and I are serious, and we're abstaining. Since we're on this topic, let me share something with you all."

Everyone stopped, and all eyes were on Todd. Feeling a little nervous, Todd cleared his throat. "I, um... I want to ask Laton to marry me."

"What?"

"Seriously?"

"Oh, that's awesome!" were the responses shared around the room.

Todd looked at Drew with questioning eyes.

"Look, Drew, I know you may not approve, but I've already spoken with Laton's parents, and they've given me the green light."

"Man, I'm not disappointed. I'm happy. I know I gave you a hard time, but that was only because she's my cousin. I knew you were playing the field, and I didn't want her to be a casualty of your game. But if you're serious—and it seems that you are—I couldn't be happier."

"Praise the Lord!" Nana Jean shouted. "Now maybe I can get some more grandbabies."

"Hold on, Mama," Todd laughed. "I haven't even proposed yet, and you're already talking about babies."

"I think I'm suddenly feeling as if I'm not enough," Trinity joked, pulling her grandmother in for a hug.

"Oh, you will always be enough, my baby girl, but grandmas are made to give that love to lots and lots of grandbabies. Just remember, you will always be my number one."

Dee sucked in a hard breath after her mom's words, not realizing everyone heard her until Drew wrapped his arm around her and asked, "Are you okay?"

"Oh, yes," she responded. "I had a twinge of heartburn and needed to burp at the same time," Dee chuckled.

"Are you sure, baby?" Nana Jean asked.

"Yes, ma'am," Dee said. "I think I'm going to fix myself a cup of tea and turn in for the night. Little brother, I am so proud of you, and I'm certain that Laton is going to say yes. Be careful getting home and let us know how we can help with the proposal."

"Will do, sis," Todd said as he hugged everyone before heading out the door.

Dee escaped to the bedroom and prepared to shower. As soon as she stepped into the shower, the tears began to fall, and she could barely catch her breath. *Why am I having this reaction now?* she thought. *It happened over sixteen years ago. It was the best decision for everyone involved. I wasn't ready. I just wasn't ready,* Dee thought as she slid to the floor of the shower, sobbing uncontrollably.

Eventually, Dee pulled herself together, got out of the shower, dried off, and put on her favorite pajamas. Just as she turned off the bathroom light and walked into the bedroom, the light from outside peeping through the blinds caught Drew's silhouette sitting on the bed.

"Oh dang, Drew, you startled me," Dee said.

"Sorry," Drew responded in a tight tone.

"What's wrong?" she asked.

"I actually need to ask you that question," Drew retorted.

"What had you crying in the shower for over thirty minutes?"

"Crying? Drew, what are you…"

"Stop it, Dee," Drew interrupted. "You and I both know you were crying. Now I want to know why."

"Drew, I… I was just emotional about the news of Todd wanting to propose to Laton. They were happy tears, I promise," Dee responded.

Drew looked at Dee with disbelief. He stood up, kissed her forehead, and said, "I'll be sleeping in the guest room downstairs until you're ready to tell me the truth."

"Drew, I am telling you the truth," Dee pleaded.

"Dee, there is no way in hell you are telling me the truth. I love you, and you know that, but I'm not going to keep rolling with this lie that everything is good with you. Goodnight. You know where I'll be when you're ready to talk."

Drew kissed Dee again and walked out the door, leaving her standing in the dark, wondering if she could, or should, tell him the truth. But telling him would change everything.

Sleep eluded Dee as she continued debating whether she should tell Drew the truth. She tossed and turned until sleep finally won out.

There was a chill in the air, and horns blared up and down the streets of New York. Dee hurried to get to class. Just as she reached the door of the building, Dee heard someone yell her name. She froze. **There's no way that's Theo.**

She heard her name again, this time closer. Dee took a deep breath and turned around, standing face-to-face with Theo.

"Oh my gosh, Theo," Dee responded, hoping he wouldn't notice she wasn't happy to see him.

"As I live and breathe, it's Deloris Bettis. How are you, girl?"

"I'm great, just running late for class. What brings you to New York?" Dee asked.

"I'm teaching an Introduction to African American Studies course at Columbia while working on my law degree. Listen, I know you have to leave, but I'd love to catch up," Theo said.

"Sure," Dee replied without thinking, just trying to end the conversation.

"What's your number?"

Dee reluctantly gave Theo her number and ran off to class. While in class, her cell phone buzzed, and she knew it had to be him, but she didn't respond. Less than five minutes later, her phone buzzed again, and she ignored it again. It happened again, and again, and again, until she finally grabbed the phone and put it on silent, but not before looking at the messages. In typical Theo fashion, the first message started light:

Hey, it was so good to see you. Drinks later? Why can't you respond? Are you seriously that busy?

Dee responded politely, **I'm in class, and yes to drinks.** As soon as she hit the send button, the voice told her to decline the meeting for drinks. But Dee ignored it and refocused her attention on her instructor.

Class finished promptly at 6:15 pm, as her instructor, the one and only formidable Dr. LaTisha Willingham, refused to be late to her spin class. She always ended her class with the following dismissal:

"See you next time, but in the meantime, be love, be light, and be you."

Dee exited the class with a group of friends who were headed to their favorite little pub down the street. She told them that she'd run into an old high school friend and was meeting him for drinks at The Ellington but would catch up with them later at the loft they all shared. They reminded her that it was Friday, and they were all going to Sydney's place in Greenwich Village. Dee had totally forgotten but agreed she would be there as soon as she was done.

As they departed, Dee heard the voice again: **Cancel the date.**

She pulled out her phone to call Theo to cancel, but as soon as she did, the phone rang, and it was him. Dee answered, and he immediately asked, "Where are you?"

She responded that she'd just gotten out of class but really needed to cancel because she had a project to work on with friends who were waiting for her. Her hair stood up on the back of her neck when Theo responded, "The friends that just went in the other direction?"

Dee froze and then turned slowly to stand face-to-face with Theo.

"Now why would you lie to me?" Theo asked.

"It wasn't a lie, per se. We do have a project, and I do need to work on it. They were just going to grab something to eat first, and I'm not hungry."

"Well, let's go have that drink, and then I'll let you get back to your little friends. It's been over five years since we've seen one another. Let's catch up," Theo said as he looped his arm around hers and waved for a taxi.

They made it to The Ellington, and as soon as they walked in, the bartender greeted Theo.

"Hey dude, where have you been? I haven't seen you in a couple of weeks."

"Work," Theo responded.

"Well, who is this beauty you have with you?"

"This is Dee, an old friend from high school that I ran into today."

"Hi," Dee said shyly.

"What would you like to drink?" Theo asked.

"Water is fine. I need to be focused on my project later."

"Seriously, Dee? One drink isn't going to hurt you."

But Dee could only think of the voice that had told her not to go.

"Yeah, I know it won't, but I really need to be clear of mind. Dr. Willingham's class is serious, and she won't accept anything less than excellence, especially from her students of color."

"I get it. I do, but it's literally one drink. I'll have my guy make it light."

"Yo, AJ!" Theo shouted. "Fix my regular for me and make the lady a lemon drop, easy on the vodka."

"You got it," AJ yelled back and started making the drinks.

"So, what have you been up to all this time?" Theo asked.

"Just school, honestly," Dee responded. "What about you?"

Theo evaded the question by asking another. "So, are you still with that dude, what's his name, Dan?"

"No, his name is Drew, and we are not together."

"Good," Theo said. "You were too good for him anyway."

"You never answered my question," Dee said. "What have you been up to?"

"School, same as you. You know I had to leave Hayward after the accusations."

"Yeah, I heard about that. Did they ever find the girl and clear your name?"

"Oh, they found her, but she wasn't able to talk because someone had strangled her to death. That's why I had to transfer."

"Oh, Theo, I'm so sorry," Dee said sympathetically. "It must have been a nightmare for you."

"She got what she deserved," Theo mumbled.

"What was that?" Dee asked.

"Oh, I said, I guess that's what I get for trying to date an upperclassman. But it all worked out for my good. I transferred to Dillard and graduated at the top of my class. Now I'm here working on my law degree and teaching."

Just as Dee was about to respond, their drinks arrived.

"One whiskey neat for the gentleman and one lemon drop for the beautiful lady. Light on the vodka," AJ said with a smile.

"Thanks," Dee said and took a sip.

"What do you think?" Theo asked.

"It's nice."

They spent the next hour just talking and catching up, which wasn't as bad as Dee had expected. As she checked her watch and realized it was almost nine, she told Theo she really enjoyed catching up but needed to leave, as her group was expecting her. Theo reluctantly agreed and paid for the drinks.

As they stood to leave, Dee stumbled.

"Hey there, girl! You are a serious lightweight. You only had one drink."

"I'm not a lightweight," she responded before looking into his eyes and passing out.

Dee sat straight up in bed, breathing hard and sweating. She pulled back the covers and went to the bathroom to wash her face.

"You have to tell," she heard the voice say.

"No! No, I will not speak of that night, ever. Please stop tormenting me. I have a good life. There's no reason to remember that time in my life."

"That time in your life created a life. You have to tell before it's too late," the voice responded.

"I can't," Dee cried.

Dee wasn't sure how long she'd sat on the floor, but she had apparently drifted off to sleep because a soft knock on the bedroom door awakened her.

"Baby girl," she heard her mom call. "Are you okay?"

Dee jumped off the floor, flushed the toilet for theatrics, and then turned on the water. She yelled out, "Come on in, Momma," as she dried her hands and walked out of the bathroom.

Nana Jean walked in with a look of concern.

"Baby, are you okay?"

"I'm fine, Momma."

"It sure didn't sound like it. I heard you crying most of the night," Nana Jean said.

"Oh, I had a bad dream, that's all. Someone was chasing me, and I was trying to get away."

"Are you sure?" Nana Jean asked.

"Yes, ma'am, I'm sure."

Dee leaned over and kissed her mother softly on the cheek.

"Is anyone else up?"

"No," Nana Jean responded, then asked, "Where is Drew?"

Dee stopped in her tracks and turned to face her mother.

"He must have fallen asleep in the media room," she said.

"Oh, okay. I just want to make sure that everything is okay with you two."

"Mom, you worry too much. Drew and I are just fine."

"Let's go make breakfast."

"Now you're speaking my language," Nana Jean chuckled.

They both walked out of Dee's bedroom, but Dee was still bothered by what the voice had told her.

"Tell, before it's too late."

Chapter 12

Over a week had gone by since the night Dee had the dream. Drew was still sleeping in the guest room, and now, not only was Nana Jean wondering what was going on, but so was Trinity.

"Mom, is there any particular reason Dad is sleeping downstairs?" Trinity asked.

"If you're asking if everything is okay with your dad and I, then the answer is yes. Your dad has been working on a major project for work, and instead of bothering me by coming to bed late, he's sleeping downstairs until it's finished," Dee responded.

Trinity knew her mom was lying because she never looked up from the magazine she was reading. It was always a telltale sign that she was withholding the truth if she didn't look at you. So, Trinity responded,

"Could you say that again, but look at me this time?"

Dee's head snapped up from the magazine, and she looked fiercely at Trinity.

"Young lady, you are treading on thin ice right about now."

"Well, I'm not," Nana Jean quipped. "So how about you look me in the face and tell me what's really going on? You and Drew have been like two ships passing in the night, and you expect us to just act as if nothing is wrong. What's wrong?"

"What's wrong?" Drew asked as he walked into the den.

"Perfect timing," Nana Jean retorted.

"For?" Drew asked tentatively.

"To explain just what the heck is going on with you and Mom," Trinity stated.

"And seeing that you two aren't talking, you haven't had a chance to get your lie together. So, Drew, you start. What's going on?"

Drew looked over at Dee with questioning eyes, almost pleading for her to give him the words to say.

"Okay," Drew said. "We've not been sleeping in the same room together because I want to have another baby and Dee doesn't."

"And there you have it, folks, another lie," Trinity said.

"Watch your mouth," they all said to her instantaneously.

"Let me get this straight," Trinity said. "You two aren't telling the truth, and we all know it, yet somehow the tables turn, and you all jump on me for saying the word 'lie'? I'm going to my room," Trinity said as she walked away. "Make it make sense, baby Jesus," she said as she continued down the hall.

"Now that she's gone, do you two care to tell the truth about what's really going on?" Nana asked.

"It's nothing. We're fine," Dee and Drew answered simultaneously.

"Well, if this is nothing and you two are fine, I'll be a monkey's uncle and his aunt, too," Nana Jean replied. She looked at them both and told them to fix it before it was too late, then walked away.

Drew and Dee just looked at one another, neither saying a word. Finally, Drew asked,

"So, what did you tell them?"

"Oh, that you were working on a project and didn't want to come to bed late and wake me up," Dee said.

"Hmm," Drew said. "So, I guess me throwing the baby talk out there really did put us in left field."

"More like showing up late to basketball practice with a baseball glove, only to realize it was actually football practice."

They both laughed and then Drew apologized for taking things too far.

Dee responded by saying words she never thought she'd utter.

"Drew, I have something to tell you."

"What is it, honey?" Drew asked. "You know you can tell me anything," he said as he sat beside her on the sofa and grabbed her hand.

"I think we need to take a ride in order to have this conversation. Mom and Trinity don't need to hear this," Dee said.

"Sure thing. When would you like to take this drive?" Drew inquired.

"Now, before I lose my nerve to tell you."

"Okay, let's go," he said.

They both got up from the sofa and headed out the door without as much as a single word to either Nana Jean or Trinity.

Drew left the house and jumped on the 417, heading nowhere in particular but steadily moving toward the I-4 exchange. After driving about 10 miles, Drew broke the silence by asking how Dee was feeling.

"Nervous," she replied.

"About?"

"About how you are going to take what I have to tell you."

"Babe, you know you can tell me anything, and it won't change how I feel about you."

"You say that now, but I'm not so sure."

Drew continued to drive but decided to pull over just as they reached Old Towne. After putting the truck in park, he turned toward Dee and grabbed her hands.

"Listen, before you say anything, let's pray."

"Dear Heavenly Father, we thank you for the many sacrifices You made that allow us to be here at this moment. Thank you for loving us in spite of our wayward ways and thoughts. Lord, we ask that as we have this conversation, we are mindful that we are Your children, and that we extend grace and mercy to one another as You have to us. May You be ever-present in all that we say and do, and may it always be pleasing unto You. It's in Your name that we pray and ask these things. Amen."

"Thank you for that," Dee said with tears in her eyes. "Drew, what I'm about to share with you is the hardest thing I've ever had to utter out of my mouth. I've never told anyone what I'm about to say to you."

Dee took a deep breath and began to recount that chilly September night back in 2001.

"Do you recall the time we were broken up while in grad school?"

"Yeah, I was an idiot and dumped you because I didn't feel you were supporting me," Drew recalled.

"Do you remember anything else about that time?" Dee asked.

"Only that by the time I came to my senses, you weren't trying to hear anything I had to say. You didn't take my calls for almost a year, and I thought I'd lost you forever. The last time we spoke before you shut me out was in the fall of 2001, I think," Drew said. "You told me that classes were great but hectic and you weren't sure if you were coming home for Thanksgiving or Christmas. Matter of fact, now that I think about it, you didn't come home at all. Your parents were even worried you were taking on too much because they could barely reach you at times."

"Well, what I'm about to tell you directly coincides with that timeframe," Dee stated. "But before I tell you, you have to promise me that you won't get angry, and you won't do anything foolish."

"What?" Drew said. "Dee, stop playing. When have I ever—"

"I'm serious, Drew," Dee interrupted. "Promise me, and don't say anything until I'm finished."

"Fine, I promise," Drew said.

Dee dove into recounting the events, starting with the last time they talked.

"As you recalled," Dee started, "we last spoke on the 13th of September. The next day, I ran into Theo Henderson, my ex-boyfriend from high school. He was in New York working on his law degree while teaching at Columbia, and he invited me out for a drink to catch up. I reluctantly agreed to go, and we went to The Ellington. We were only there for about an hour and a half, and I only had one drink, a lemon drop. The drink tasted absolutely fine, and I'd asked the bartender to go light on the vodka. However, when I got up to leave, the room started to spin, and I blacked out. That was the last thing I remember until the next day around noon. I was supposed to meet the group at Sydney's place in Greenwich Village, but I never made it. They were the ones who woke me up the next day, asking why I didn't show up. When I looked at my phone, I saw that I'd missed multiple calls from them, and a text from Theo saying he had a nice time and hoped we could do it again. I remember being really sore, but I do not recall why. It wasn't until my roommate, Tammy, asked me how I got the bruise on the back of my neck that it all came rushing back to me."

"I immediately told her that I'd fallen down some steps and that was why I didn't show up — because I'd passed out from bumping my head and was sorry for not calling. They wanted to take me to the hospital to get checked, but I told them that I'd already been."

"It was a few days later before I could actually say the words that I'm about to say to you, to myself," Dee said. "Theo raped me. I recall him putting me in a taxi and taking me to some dark warehouse-type place. I kept telling him I really needed to go, and he said not until I gave him what I owed him all those years ago. He tied my hands up above my head to some type of bar, and then he tied each of my legs to a pole after he took my shoes and jeans off. He raped me repeatedly until I passed out again. I can remember his breath smelling like whiskey, and how he kept trying to make me kiss him. When I refused, he grabbed my hair and banged my head against the pole, and that's how I got the bruise on the back of my neck that Tammy saw."

"After what felt like an eternity, Theo dressed me and brought me back to the school and dropped me off. I walked back to the loft, showered, and scrubbed every inch of my body until it was red. Then, I got into the bed, hoping that it was all a bad dream."

"I tried to act normal by going to class and keeping up my regular schedule, but I was paranoid. I was jumping at the slightest thing, hoping that I'd never hear from him or see him again, and I didn't. But just when I felt like I could breathe again — which was like six months later — I found out I was pregnant. I went to the school infirmary because I thought I had food poisoning or the flu, but it turned out I had a life inside me."

"Being that I had broken up with you and the only other person I had been with had raped me, I knew it was Theo's baby. I couldn't abort, so I hid the little weight gain I had and found an agency that would allow me to anonymously give the baby up for adoption. He was born on June 30, 2002, weighing 8 pounds, 12 ounces, and was 22 inches long. Because I was giving him up, I didn't name him, and I never held him, but I did see him. As perfect as he was, he had his father's eyes. The eyes of a rapist."

"I went back to school a week later and finished up my summer courses, and no one was aware. No one expected that I was going through the most traumatic episode ever, or that I'd just given birth, or that I blamed myself for it all. Because I should have said no. No to the invitation. No to the drink. Just no."

Dee drew in one final breath and said, "No one knew any of that, and no one knows that I killed Theo because of what he did to me. That's it. That's all. That's the secret I've been holding from you for over sixteen years." Then Dee exhaled.

Drew sat in stark silence, with tears rolling down his face. Unable to speak, he grabbed Dee's face and kissed her on both cheeks. As he held her, Dee could faintly hear him saying, "I'm so sorry. If I hadn't been such a jerk about you supporting me, this wouldn't have happened."

"Are you sure you killed him?" Drew asked.

"What?" Dee responded in bewilderment. "What kind of question is that?"

"Because if you didn't, I'm going to," Drew answered.

As the headlights from a passing car lit up the interior of the truck, it was at that moment Dee could see that Drew was clenching his jaw—something he only did when he was furious.

"Let's get home," Drew finally spoke. "I don't want Nana and Trinity to start worrying."

"Okay," Dee said. "But since we're here at Old Towne, can I get a funnel cake first?"

"Dee!" Drew exclaimed. "You just told me you killed someone, and you want a funnel cake? Girl, you are wild."

"Come on, let's get this funnel cake and get home," Drew said with a grin as they exited the truck. But in the back of his mind, he was planning to verify if Theo was really dead. Because if he wasn't, he was going to make sure that he ended up that way.

Chapter 13

Months had passed since Dee shared with Drew the details of that night, and he hadn't asked another question. He wasn't distant, but she knew it had changed him in some way. They still had their Thursday night dates, and they were always full of fun and excitement, but Dee could tell something was different about Drew. She wanted to ask, but she was afraid of what he might say. Would he want to separate, or worse, divorce? As much as she tried not to think about it, it was very difficult. Thankfully, she had Trinity's birthday party plans to keep her busy. They were doing much more than they typically would, given that her past few parties had been surrounded by turmoil. And although it wasn't her sixteenth birthday, they were definitely going all out as if it were. In the grand scheme of things, fourteen was a big deal, considering everything.

Dee was deep into party planning mode when she heard music in the background. *Don't know what I'd ever do without you, from the beginning to the end.* Dee smiled because she knew it was Carmen calling. That was their ringtone for one another.

"Hey, friend," Dee said as soon as she hit the talk button.

"Hey, girl," Carmen responded. "How are the party plans coming, and what do you need from me?"

"The plans are coming along just fine. I've booked three hours at Nona Park Adventures where everyone is invited to attend. After that, Trinity and the girls will have their spa treatments and hair styled by Stacy's salon girls. I think Drew said he and Curtis, Jerome, and Todd were taking the boys golfing and then for haircuts. They will have an early dinner at Le Coq Au Vin Deuce and then party the night away at the clubhouse."

"Dee, that sounds amazing," Carmen said. "One question."

"What's that?" Dee chimed.

"Did you remember to book the limo?"

"Shoot! I totally forgot about that part. I hope I can get a reservation with such short notice."

"No worries," Carmen replied. "I figured you had forgotten when we talked on Tuesday, so I called and reserved it to pick all the kids up from your place at six."

"See, just like Brandy said, I don't know what I'd do without you." They both laughed, and Dee ended the call as she heard Drew coming into the house.

"I'll holler at you later."

"Okay, bye," Carmen said, and they both hung up.

Drew came into the kitchen from the mudroom and noticed there was no one around, which was strange because Nana was always in or near the kitchen.

"Hey," he called. "Where is everyone?"

"I'm in the study," Dee called back.

Moments later, Drew appeared in the doorway with a smile and flowers.

"Hey, babe," he said. "This is for you."

"Oh, Drew, you are something special, you know. What are these for?" Dee questioned.

"Just because I love you so much," Drew replied. "Where are Nana and Trinity?"

"Mom is with Retha at the clubhouse, remember? Today was the start of water aerobics."

"Oh yeah, I totally forgot about that. I'm actually surprised she agreed to go. You know Nana ain't about getting her hair wet."

They both laughed and walked out of the study toward the kitchen. As Dee put the fresh flowers into a clean vase, she told Drew that Trinity was at violin practice and would catch a ride home with either Ian or Keisha, as they both had class today.

"So what you're saying is we're all alone in this big ol' house and can do whatever we want?" Drew said in his sultry voice as he glided behind Dee and wrapped his arms around her waist.

"Well, that wasn't what I was saying, but I definitely like your idea of how to spend the time," Dee said as she turned and met her lips with his.

Just as they were preparing to turn things up a notch, the doorbell rang. Drew pulled away to go see who was at the door, but Dee pulled him back and instructed him to ignore it.

"Yes, ma'am," he said with a grin while scooping her up and heading down the hallway.

They were awakened a few hours later by Trinity knocking at their door. Dee told her to come in, and Trinity immediately burst into the room but stopped short when she realized they were in bed.

"Wait. Why are you two in the bed and it's only five o'clock?"

"Well, if it's any of your business, ma'am," Drew interjected, "I was tired from the project I've been working on for the past four months and wanted to take a well-deserved nap. Your mom decided to join me because she's been busy with your birthday plans."

"Yeah, about that," Trinity said. "I was wondering if we could have dinner at Flemings instead of Le Coq Au Vin Deuce."

"Why?" Dee groaned. "Do you know how hard it is to get reservations there?"

"Yes, ma'am, I do. It's just that… never mind, it's okay. Let's just stick with that," Trinity said as she dropped her head and turned to leave.

As she started toward the door, Dee heard the voice say, *"Change the venue."*

"Wait, wait," Dee said. "We will change the venue to Flemings."

"Really?" Trinity said with her face all aglow.

"Yes," Dee responded.

"Thanks, Mom. Thanks, Dad." And out the room she ran, likely to call her friends.

"I wonder what that was all about," Drew inquired.

"Hmm, who knows?" said Dee. "Teenage angst, likely," although she knew it was more, because she had heard the voice.

"I need to prepare dinner, so let's get up," Dee said.

"How about we order in for Trinity and Nana and resume our previous activities?" Drew stated as he pulled Dee back onto the bed.

"Boy, stop," Dee laughed. "You and I both know we'd never hear the end of it from Mom if we ordered out in the middle of the week."

"Touché, my dear. Touché. Let us prepare ourselves to cook dinner, and by 'us,' I mean *you*," teased Drew.

"I'm not above bribing you, sir. Either you help me, or I'll tell Mom why dinner is late tonight."

"Ooh, hitting below the belt, I see. Well, since I don't want my beloved mother-in-law to know all the things I did to you, I will reluctantly help you with dinner," Drew laughed and went into the bathroom for a quick shower.

Dee laid in the bed for a few more minutes before heading into the bathroom herself. Just long enough to wonder what Trinity heard or saw that made her want to change venues. She planned to approach the matter with her but wanted to get past the festivities first. But would inquiring about the premonitions force her to reveal things about herself? She had already come clean about something in her past with Drew that she'd never planned to tell. She didn't want that to be the case with Trinity, but she wasn't sure if she could continue to act as if she wasn't aware.

Chapter 14

Excitement was in full bloom as the birthday festivities were set to kick off promptly at nine Saturday morning. All of the girls were staying the night with Trinity, so the moms decided they'd stay over to help. Stacy called around midday to say that Kingston's mom, Jewel, wanted to come over since all the boys were staying at her home, and there was no way she wanted to try and survive all of the testosterone. Dee laughed and told Stacy to bring Jewel over. Jewel and Dee hadn't spent a lot of time together, but what better time than this, especially since her son was dating Dee's daughter?

Dee called Carmen, who in turn called Stacy so she could gather intel on Jewel and her husband Micah. From their conversation, Dee learned that they relocated from New Jersey when Jewel was offered the Head of Obstetrics and Gynecology position at UCF Lake Nona Hospital. Her husband, Micah, was also an OB-GYN and worked alongside her at the clinic they opened shortly after moving. They had twin girls, age 8, and a son they adopted, who's 18 and attended Bethune-Cookman University. Dee also found out that they were the family building the massive home around the corner from her and Carmen. They had only settled in their current home because they needed to move quickly, and the new construction wouldn't have been finished in time. As she got off the phone with her girls, Dee smiled to herself, thinking that her daughter had good taste, just like her.

Saturday morning came early—too early for all the moms, as it seemed the girls didn't fall asleep until well after two a.m., and here they were at six o'clock, making enough noise to rival a chainsaw. By the time all the moms were up and moving, Nana Jean had already corralled the girls into the kitchen for a light breakfast of fruit, bagels, yogurt, and juice. Keisha was very adamant that she would have preferred Nana's homemade waffles but was quickly reminded that she was about to head to the amusement park and didn't need anything heavy on her stomach. The exact words Nana Jean told her were, "Baby, people all over the world have wants, and yet, they still manage to carry on when they don't get them." The girls snickered, and Keisha rolled her eyes at them, which only made them burst into full-blown laughter.

As soon as they were done with breakfast and everyone was dressed, they loaded up the cars and headed to Nona Adventure Park. Nana Jean and Gigi Retha stayed behind to clean up and make sure everything was ready when the kids returned from the park.

"Honey, these kids sure know how to party," Jean said.

"Who are you telling?" replied Retha. "At least your room was upstairs, away from the noise. Those girls snickered and giggled into the wee hours of the morning. And they stayed on those phones talking to those boys. I think Dee finally took their phones around one this morning."

"Baby, I was deep in my sleep," Jean said.

"I told you to sleep in Trinity's room, but you're nosey and had to be down in the midst of the fray. Now look at you. Tired."

They both laughed as Retha agreed with everything Jean had said.

"These kids are mighty blessed, you know?" Jean said.

"Yes, indeed they are," Retha answered.

"I don't think in my wildest dreams I ever imagined that my children or theirs would be living this grand of a life. I mean, David and I always wanted the best for them and did the best we could to provide, but this..." Jean stopped talking as she got choked up. While dabbing at the tears streaming down her face, she continued, "This is more than I could ever imagine."

Retha agreed, tears falling from her eyes as well. "You know, I didn't even think I'd be here to see any of this," she said. "God has been mighty good to us both."

"Yes, He has truly been good," Jean said. "Better than good."

They hugged and then finished cleaning the kitchen and the downstairs area, so they'd be ready when everyone returned. In fact, they finished quickly enough that they both had the opportunity to take a nap and were just waking up when the kids came bursting through the door, full of chatter, shortly after noon.

"Girl, did you see how Reggie and Sullivan flew off the slide at the Aqua Park?" Keisha laughed.

"Hey now, you can lay off my boo," Catrina said with a snap of her finger and a roll of her neck. Everyone turned and looked at her, then instantly burst into laughter.

"Baby, both of them came flying off that slide like wet noodles," Camille snorted.

"Hey, Nana. Hey, Gigi," all the girls said as they realized they were in their presence.

"Hey, girls," they responded.

"I take it that a good time was had?" Nana Jean asked.

"Was it ever!" Trinity responded. "I think this has been one of the best birthdays ever, and it's just getting started." She gave her Nana and

Gigi a hug and then headed down the hall to catch up with the others who had already gone to her room.

"I remember having energy like that," Retha said with a smile.

"Me too, honey, me too," Jean replied.

As soon as they readied themselves to sit down in the den, Dee, Stacy, and Carmen came through the door.

"I need a shot of tequila, a shower, and a nap," Dee said.

"In that specific order," Stacy said as she closed the door.

"Well, did you ladies have fun?" Retha inquired.

"Define fun, exactly," Carmen retorted.

They all laughed and sat down to relax for a while. There was a brief recap of the events at the park, and then things went quiet as Dee, Stacy, and Carmen all fell asleep. Jean and Retha covered each of them with a throw blanket and went out onto the patio to relax until it was time for the next phase of activities.

Exactly two hours later, the house was in full bloom once again with the laughter of teenage girls and worn-out mothers. Stacy's salon girls had pampered Trinity and her friends as if they were royalty, and they were all the more wired for it. Now it was 5:00, and they were rushing to get ready for dinner at six.

"You have five minutes!" Stacy yelled.

"Dinner isn't until six," Jewel said with more of a question in her voice than a statement.

"If we don't hurry these girls up, they'll miss dinner," Stacy responded as she looked over at Jewel.

Jewel smiled and said, "So this is what I have to look forward to in the next few years?"

"You have no idea," replied Carmen.

"Times two at the same time," Dee chimed in.

"Please don't remind me," Jewel stated.

Trinity ran into the media room where the ladies were all gathered.

"Mom, can you zip me up?"

"Um, excuse you, miss," Dee admonished. "Did you not hear us talking?"

"Oh, sorry," Trinity said. "Excuse me."

She stated, "Yes, ma'am, how may I assist you?"

"Can you zip me up, please?" Trinity asked.

Dee zipped Trinity's dress and told her to gather the girls and head outside.

After what felt like an eternity to the mothers, the girls finally made it outside, just as the limo pulled up. The girls all squealed at the realization that this would be their ride for the evening.

"Thanks, Mom," Trinity said as she fought back tears. "This has been the best birthday ever."

"You're welcome, honey," Dee said as she, too, fought back tears. "Come on, let's get you all inside."

The limo driver held the door open as the girls all climbed inside. After they were settled, he closed the door and headed to the driver's seat. Just as he opened his door, he made eye contact with Dee, and she froze. It was apparently long enough that Stacy and Carmen had to snap her out of her daze.

"Girl, what is going on with you?" Carmen asked.

"Chile, I must have fallen asleep because this day has worn me out," Dee clamored quickly.

"Well, you look like you've seen a ghost," Stacy responded.

A ghost, indeed, Dee thought to herself. *Those eyes. I'll never forget those eyes, but there's no way. Absolutely no way*, Dee said to herself—or so she thought.

"No way what?" Nana Jean asked as she walked up to get into the SUV.

"No way that my baby is turning fourteen."

"Baby, with the amount of money y'all have shelled out, you would think today was her wedding day," Jean said with a huff as she pulled herself up into the Range Rover.

"Mom, don't start," Dee replied.

"I haven't started anything; I'm merely stating a fact."

"Very true," Dee agreed. "But after all she's endured the past two years or so, don't you think we owed her this?"

"I suppose, but sometimes you and Drew have a tendency to go overboard, that's all."

"Now come on here before we're late, because I'm hungry," Jean snapped as she closed the door.

"Yes ma'am," Dee said with a chuckle as she rounded the back of the SUV to get in the driver's seat. As she buckled her seatbelt, she heard the voice say, "*You know what you saw,*" and the hair on the back of her neck stood up as she started the SUV.

Dee maneuvered through traffic quickly and quietly. Too quiet for Nana Jean.

"What's wrong, baby?" she asked.

"Oh, nothing. Just thinking about what you said," Dee responded, all the while hoping her mom didn't notice that she was lying.

"Listen, Dee, I didn't say that to make you feel away about what you do for Trinity. I said it because I want you to stay mindful that you teach her to always be respectful, loving, and caring of others. Especially those who are less fortunate. And not to take these things for granted because she's not entitled to anything in life—she has to earn it like everyone else."

"Mom, I know," Dee said, sounding much like a little girl in her reply. "I was just hoping that you weren't thinking that I had thrown my upbringing out the window. I promise I am instilling in her everything you instilled in Todd and me."

"Never," Jean said as they pulled up to the restaurant, just as the girls were getting out of the limo.

"The kids had a marvelous time at dinner, but they were definitely ready for the final turn-up of the night at the clubhouse," Drew said.

"Man, listen," Curtis said, "I'm going to need a few days off behind this. These kids have been on ten all day!"

Terrell, Todd, and Micah all agreed with a head nod.

"Come on, let's get them loaded up in this limo and back to the clubhouse," Drew stated.

Just as he was turning to motion for the kids, there was a loud boom, and the earth literally shook. All the kids began screaming, and everyone ducked down because they weren't sure what was going on at the time.

Eventually, Todd noticed a large cloud of smoke billowing into the air. As he looked in the direction of the smoke and started to stand, there was another explosion. Retha and Jean quickly gathered the kids and put them into the limo. They told Stacy and Dee they would meet them at the house with the kids.

As the limo began pulling off, Dee heard the voice say, *"Le Coq..."*

Just as Trinity stuck her head out the window of the limo and finished with, "Au Vin Deuce."

"Le Coq Au Vin Deuce," Dee whispered.

Carmen and Stacy turned to her and asked what she was talking about. Dee responded that they needed to go before traffic got any worse, as they could hear all the sirens blaring and people gathering from the many restaurants and stores in the area.

Chapter 15

It was a little while later, and Trinity and her friends were enjoying the party, but it seemed that some of the excitement had worn off due to the explosion. Dee heard someone speaking to her from behind, and she didn't recognize the voice. As she turned, she realized it was the limo driver they had hired for the night.

"Oh, hi," Dee stammered, caught off guard. "Thankfully, this party is winding down because I'm exhausted," she chuckled nervously. Dee wasn't sure why she was so bothered by his presence, especially since she didn't even know him.

"What's your name, young man?" she asked.

"It's Theron. Theron Je'Haven Henderson, ma'am. But everyone calls me TJ."

"Well! What a stately name, Mr. TJ. However, I must ask—do you automatically state your full name to everyone you meet?" Dee inquired.

"No ma'am," TJ smirked. "Just those that are like family."

Dee froze, not quite understanding.

TJ noticed her uneasiness and explained, "I'm Kingston's older brother."

"Oh, my goodness!" Dee exclaimed, still shaken. She couldn't get the familiarity of his eyes out of her mind. "You've been working all night and didn't tell us? I thought you were away at school."

"Yes ma'am, I was, but classes ended a few days ago, and I decided to come home. This job kind of just landed in my lap. Imagine my surprise when I saw my family tonight."

TJ was about to say more but stopped as the kids started spilling out of the clubhouse. "Well, Mrs. Gorden, it was nice to make your acquaintance, but I think I'm now officially back on duty."

TJ walked away, and Dee just stood there. *Why do his eyes remind me of Theo's?*

Dee was admittedly shaken by what she had seen, and even more so by the realization that was etching itself in her mind. *There is absolutely no way he could be who he looks to be,* she thought to herself. But Dee couldn't allow herself to fall further down the rabbit hole of exactly who TJ was—or wasn't. She had to get back to the clubhouse to help clean, and she had to be present in the moment lest she risk Drew, or better still, her mom figuring out that she was off-kilter.

As she made her way back inside, she made a mental note to try and find out exactly where TJ was born and his birthday. However, the uneasiness would not pass her by. After all she had done to erase that traumatic time from her past, it seemed to be staring her right in the face. It was as if Theo was back from the dead, wreaking havoc in her life all over again. Dee shuddered at the thought, closed her eyes, and took a deep breath before opening the door to the clubhouse.

Chapter 16

"Home, sweet home!" Nana Jean exclaimed. "Yes, Lord, I have never been so ready to get off my feet and go to bed in a mighty long time." She walked down the hall toward her bedroom.

"Mom and Dad," Trinity chimed. "This was absolutely the best day ever! I can't imagine how you're going to top this for my Sweet 16."

"Ugh, don't remind us," Drew said. "Girl, go to bed. We just spent the equivalent of a small used car for this day, and you're already talking two years down the road."

Dee scoffed. "Kid, I love you. I really do, but you are truly doing too much right now. Good night and know that we love you dearly."

"Good night, Mom," Trinity said while hugging her, then her dad. "But seriously, you need to start planning," she teased before running off down the hall.

Dee turned and looked at Drew with a look of utter disgust.

"Why are you looking at me like that?" he asked. "I haven't said a word."

"That girl is just like you," she replied. "Head in the clouds, always trying to raise the stakes."

"Well, what can I say?" Drew smirked. "I'm good at what I do."

They both laughed and walked toward their bedroom.

Before heading to bed, Dee peeked in on her mom, who was sitting up watching TV in her bedroom.

"Hey, Mom," Dee said.

"Hey, baby, what's up?"

"Not much, I just wanted to check in on you before I go to sleep."

"Umm-hmm. Now tell me the truth," Jean said.

"You know me so well," Dee laughed.

"Yes, I do," Jean replied.

"So let's hear it. Did you get a chance to talk with the limo driver tonight?"

"You talking about TJ?"

"Umm, yes. How do you know his name?"

"Because I asked," Jean retorted. "Why?"

"No reason. I had the chance to talk with him, and he's a really nice young man. Not to mention, he's Kingston's older brother."

"Yes, he is very nice and handsome, too," Jean laughed. "And his eyes reminded me of Theo's."

Upon hearing that comment, Dee's blood ran cold. "You think so?" she muttered. "I didn't really notice."

Knowing full well that she did notice, Dee was surprised that her mom had as well.

"Honey, you must not have looked at him at all. If I were a betting woman, I'd say Theo was that boy's daddy. I mean, they did adopt him," Jean said while looking at the TV, not noticing that Dee had passed out.

After getting no response, Jean turned around to see Dee crumpled on the floor. "Lord Jesus!" she shouted.

Jean jumped up and ran to the hallway, screaming Drew's name. "Drew! Drewwww!" she called. "Lord help my baby. Drew!"

Finally, Drew and Trinity appeared in the hallway.

"What's wrong, Nana?"

"It's Dee, she's passed out or something," Jean stammered.

Drew flew past Nana Jean to find Dee in a heap on the floor. He called her name, but she didn't answer. Drew checked for a pulse, and it was faint, as was her breathing.

"Trinity, call 911 and your Aunt Carmen."

"Yes, sir," Trinity mumbled through tears in her eyes. "What's wrong with Mommy?" she asked Nana Jean.

"I don't know, honey, but she's going to be okay. God's got her," she replied.

Carmen and Curtis pulled up just as the ambulance arrived. Trinity ran to Camille with tears in her eyes. "I don't want my mom to die," she sobbed.

Camille grabbed her friend by the hand and immediately began to pray. It seemed as if an eternity had passed before the paramedics came out of the house with Dee on the gurney, still unresponsive.

"Trinity, stay with your Nana, and I'll call as soon as I know something," Drew shouted as he ran to his truck. "Your Uncle Todd is on the way."

"Yes, sir," Trinity managed to say, barely above a whisper.

"I'll stay with them, and Curtis, you go with Drew," Carmen said.

The driver of the ambulance hit the siren, and it scared Trinity to the point of hysteria. She began running down the driveway toward it, calling for her mom.

Carmen caught her and urged her back to the house, telling her everything would be okay.

As minutes turned to hours, they all sat around waiting. Nana Jean prayed constantly and was a pillar of strength, even though she was surely beyond worried on the inside. By the time the three-hour mark of waiting had passed, the house was full of people. Uncle Todd and Laton, Stacy and Terrell, Jewel and Micah, and all of Trinity's friends were there. Jerome had gone to the hospital to be with Drew and Curtis. Everything seemed normal, except it wasn't. They still didn't have an understanding of what was going on with Dee.

"Drew, please sit down," Curtis said. "You're going to wear a hole in the floor."

"Man, they aren't telling me anything, and it's driving me insane," Drew responded.

"I understand, but pacing isn't going to make it better. Besides, we need to remain positive that no news is good news."

"That's very true," Jerome chimed in, trying to sound chipper, although he was worried.

"I hear you. I do, but it's been three hours. What could they be doing that has taken three hours?" Drew questioned.

There were doctors and nurses everywhere. Machines were beeping, and Dee could see and hear it all; she just couldn't respond. She watched as her body lay cold and lifeless, but the machine showed her heart rate.

"Wake up," she whispered.

"Not yet," the voice answered.

"Wait! What do you mean, not yet?" Dee questioned.

"Come with me," the voice beckoned.

"No! I'm not ready to die," Dee stammered.

"Come," the voice said again.

But before Dee could protest further, she found herself in the delivery room where she had given birth eighteen years earlier.

As she hovered above the action, she was able to notice things she hadn't noticed the day she gave birth. There was a young doctor in training in the room. She was thin, with long black hair, and almond-shaped eyes the color of pecans.

"Is that? It can't be. That's Jewel," Dee was shocked. "How did she...? Why?"

"I don't understand," she said.

"Come," the voice said again.

This time, they were in the stairwell. As Dee watched, she saw Jewel make a phone call. It was what she heard that made her hold her breath.

"Hey, babe," Jewel said, "If you are still interested in adopting, I just found us the perfect baby. He was just born to a young mother who was the victim of a rape, and she doesn't want to keep him. He is perfect in every way. His eyes are the most glorious shade of hazel green I've ever seen."

Silence. A head nod.

"And then," Jewel said, "I'll get the paperwork from the head nurse tonight. Can you believe it? If this goes well, we will be parents. Albeit young parents, as we are only twenty-six years old. We aren't much older than the birth mother, but I believe this is the right thing to do. It just feels right, Micah."

"Yes," Jewel replied to whatever Micah said on the other side of the phone. "I love you, too. See you tonight," and she ended the call.

Just as Dee was about to question what was happening, she heard urgent, tense voices.

"She's coding! Someone please call a code blue and get Dr. Hinton in here stat!"

Dee looked around as she heard "code blue" being called and realized it was for her. As she hovered over her body, she saw the doctors and nurses working frantically. She heard words like "v-fib" and "epi" before everyone stood back as Dr. Hinton looked at the clock and said, "Time of…"

"No! No, no, no!" Dee screamed. "I can't die. I can't leave my family. Please!" she cried.

Then she heard the voice say, *"Go back."*

Dee hurried back to her body, and as her soul settled, she took in an exaggerated breath, much to the doctors' and nurses' surprise.

A nurse put an oxygen mask over her face, which Dee immediately pulled off. As they tried to explain to her that she needed the oxygen, she managed to whisper Drew's name.

Dr. Hinton told her not to worry, that she would see him soon, but they needed to make sure she was okay. Dee nodded and then dozed off as the nurse administered something through her IV.

Just as Drew was nearing the end of his rope while waiting, Dr. Hinton appeared.

"Mr. Gorden," she asked.

"Yes, that's me, but please call me Drew."

"Hello, Drew. I'm Dr. Hinton, and I've been working with your wife tonight."

"Is she okay? What's going on? Why has it taken so long?"

"Please, let's take a seat, and I'll bring you up to speed on everything. As you know, your wife was unconscious when she arrived in the ER. She remained so for some time, but her vitals were good, so we focused on trying to determine why she wasn't responding to any stimuli. During the various tests, her vitals took a dive, and she coded."

"Coded? Are you trying to tell me that my wife is dead?"

"Mr. Gorden, your wife coded, and we took all life-saving measures but were unsuccessful. However, just as we were about to call time of death, she regained consciousness."

"Oh, thank God," Drew exhaled. "When can I see her?"

"Soon. They're just waiting to put her in a room where we will continue to monitor her."

After Dr. Hinton walked away, Drew collapsed under the weight of everything he'd heard, but Curtis and Jerome were there to catch him.

"Hey, man," Jerome said. "She's okay. Don't focus on anything else that the doctor said, you hear me? Dee is okay."

"Yes, Dee is okay," Curtis chimed in, with tears in his eyes. "You need to get yourself together before you call Nana Jean and Trinity and definitely before you head back to see Dee."

"Thanks, guys, you're both right," Drew said as he stood up, wiped his face, and pulled his phone out of his pocket to call home.

Drew called and told Nana Jean and Trinity everything except the part about Dee dying. They were ecstatic and wanted to know when they could come to the hospital. Drew told them he thought the next day would be better since they were just getting her to a room and wanted her to rest. He told Nana Jean he'd stay the night and return in the morning to pick them up. Just as he was ending the call, a nurse appeared to tell him that Dee had been moved to her room and gave him the room number.

"Eighth floor, room 8176."

"Eighth floor, room 8176," Drew kept repeating to himself as he rode the elevator.

As soon as he walked into the room, he stopped short when he saw all of the tubes and machines. Dee was lying there, looking so pale and small in that moment, that Drew promised himself and God he'd never leave her side. He grabbed a chair, put it next to the bed, and sat down. As he took her hand, he kissed it and called her name.

Dee opened her eyes and spoke only four words that would change their lives forever.

"TJ is my son."

ABOUT THE AUTHOR

K. L. is a passionate storyteller and dedicated community advocate who can often be found crafting, engaging in local outreach, or immersing herself in creative pursuits. Writing a novel was always on her list of life goals, and with *Moved by the Whispers*, that dream became a reality.

By day, she fights crime as a skilled fraud investigator, and by night, she finds solace in faith, family, and the written word. A devoted student of the Bible, K. L. cherishes moments spent studying scripture, cooking up delicious meals, and creating lasting memories with loved ones. Any free time she thinks she has is quickly claimed by her beloved niece and nephews—her "unemployed besties"—who keep her on her toes with their endless energy and laughter.

Rooted in Alabama and surrounded by family, K. L. embraces life with an adventurous spirit, traveling whenever her schedule allows. Whether she's penning her next novel, exploring new destinations, or making a difference in her community, she approaches every endeavor with heart, purpose, and a commitment to leaving a lasting impact.

ACKNOWLEDGMENT

To those I love, know that I love you deeply. The completion of this book would not have been possible without your unwavering support, constant encouragement, and invaluable feedback. I would like to express my deepest gratitude and appreciation to the following:

Mom, for your unshakeable love and devotion, and for the countless, unspoken words of encouragement. Most of all, thank you for allowing me the honor of hearing your heart from the inside. I hope I have been the answer to some of your wildest dreams.

Kenya, Kendra, Cheryl, and Andora, for never allowing me to give up on bringing this book to life. Your consistent inquiries for more chapters and your steadfast belief in me helped more than you'll ever truly know. Your honest feedback has shaped this book into something I believe is truly special. Thank you for always keeping it real.

To all my remaining relatives, friends, naysayers, and others – thank you for the diverse roles you played in bringing me to this moment.

Above all, to my Heavenly Father, the giver of wisdom, grace, and love. But the greatest of these is love! I love You, God, because You first loved me. Thank you.

Made in the USA
Columbia, SC
07 June 2025